"THE MOST VITALLY ENTERTAINING MUSICAL IN MANY A BROADWAY SEASON."
—*Rolling Stone*

"*Falsettos* is not only the best new Broadway musical of the season, but shows that the American musical can take on serious issues without being trivial or losing pizazz. . . . Nobody since Leonard Bernstein has captured American vernacular speech rhythms with such precision as Finn. . . . A musical and dramatic Broadway landmark." —*USA Today*

"To call *Falsettos* a musical about gay life in modern times is also to shortchange its tremendous appeal as a masterly feat of comic storytelling and as a visionary musical theater work." —*Variety*

"A picture of our jumbled society, where lesbian kosher caterers and bar mitzvahs in AIDS wards with shrinks officiating aren't just cute anomalies, but signs of the paradox in which we live. . . . Finn's neatly askew song-play is too smart to attempt answers; its success is in phrasing the questions so poignantly." —*The Village Voice*

WILLIAM FINN received two 1992 Tony Awards for Best Score and Best Book for *Falsettos*. He has also won the Outer Critics Circle Award for Best Musical and two Los Angeles Drama Critics Awards.

JAMES LAPINE collaborated with Stephen Sondheim on *Sunday in the Park with George* (for which he was co-winner of the Pulitzer Prize) and *Into the Woods*. With Finn, Lapine received the 1992 Tony Award for Best Book for *Falsettos*. Both authors live in New York City.

FALSETTOS

"FALSETTOS"
"March of the Falsettos"
and
"Falsettoland"

by William Finn and James Lapine

and

"IN TROUSERS"

by William Finn

With an Afterword by Frank Rich

A PLUME BOOK

REGISTERED TRADEMARK—MARCA REGISTRADA

LIBRARY OF CONGRESS CATALOGING IN PUBLICATION DATA

Finn, William.
   [Musicals. Librettos. Selections]
   Falsettos : three one-act musicals / William Finn and James Lapine; with an afterword by Frank Rich.
      p.   cm.
   Contents: In trousers—March of the falsettos—Falsettoland.
   ISBN 0-452-27072-3
   1. Musicals—Librettos. I. Lapine, James. II. Title.
ML49.F55R5   1993 <Case>
782.1'4'0268—dc20   92-45275
                                                      CIP
                                                      MN

Printed in the United States of America
Set in Century Expanded

PUBLISHER'S NOTE

This is a work of fiction. Names, characters, places, and incidents either are the product of the author's imagination or are used fictitiously, and any resemblance to actual persons, living or dead, events, or locales is entirely coincidental.

CONTENTS

AUTHOR'S NOTE

Originally these three shows were intended as a trilogy, to be done, I thought, in one night. That is, as I wrote "In Trousers" and became friendly with the characters, I hoped they'd hang around for a while. So I wrote "March of the Falsettos" with James Lapine, in which the canvas of characters expanded, and six years later began work on "Falsettoland." (So there was my trilogy.) The "Falsettos" seen on Broadway is a combination, with adjustments, of "March of the Falsettos" and "Falsettoland." Since it's the best-known by-product of all these works and probably the reason you're buying this volume (or merely skimming in the bookstore—which is all right too), Lapine and I decided to put "Falsettos" first, much to the chagrin of our esteemed editor, Matthew Carnicelli. But to our minds "Falsettos" is the real event of the book, and the terminally confusing "In Trousers" an exhilarating sideshow. So be it.

First: "Falsettos." Second: "In Trousers." Third: Frank Rich's piece about bringing his young sons to see "Falsettos." (I wanted it here.)

And finally: For James Lapine, and for the Weisslers, who produced "Falsettos," I especially want to thank our superb cast, and to dedicate this volume to Michael Rupert, Stephen Bogardus, and Chip Zien, who have stayed with these shows—off and on—for eleven years, an act of love and folly I do not hesitate to get stupid about. But guys, I regret it's only paperback.

William Finn
February 28, 1993

"FALSETTOS"

"March of the Falsettos"

and

"Falsettoland"

The Broadway production of "FALSETTOS" opened at the John Golden Theatre on April 29, 1992. It was directed by James Lapine, and produced by Barry and Fran Weissler; Alecia Parker was the associate producer. The set was designed by Douglas Stein, the costumes by Ann Hould-Ward, and the lighting by Frances Aronson. Musical arrangement was by Michael Starobin, musical direction by Scott Frankel, and sound design by Peter Fitzgerald. The cast was as follows:

Marvin.. Michael Rupert
Whizzer..Stephen Bogardus
Mendel.. Chip Zien
Jason ....Jonathan Kaplan
Jason (Wed. & Sat. matinees).. Andrew Harrison Leeds
Trina .... Barbara Walsh
Charlotte...................................... Heather MacRae
Cordelia ....Carolee Carmello

March of the Falsettos

For Andre Bishop and Michael Starobin

"March of the Falsettos," originally produced in 1981 by Playwrights Horizons under the artistic direction of Andre Bishop, was subsequently produced in New York by Warner Theatre Productions, Inc., Coth Enterprises, Ltd., and the Whole Picture Co., Ltd. It was directed by James Lapine. The set was designed by Douglas Stein, the costumes by Maureen Connor and the lighting by Frances Aronson. Vocal arrangements were by William Finn, Alison Fraser, and Michael Starobin. Mr. Starobin was also the orchestrator and musical director. The production stage manager was Johnna Murray. The cast was as follows:

Marvin .... Michael Rupert
Trina, his ex-wife .... Alison Fraser
Jason, his son .... James Kushner
Whizzer Brown, his lover .... Stephen Bogardus
Mendel, his psychiatrist .... Chip Zien

(All the furniture is on wheels. Locations change in the blink of an eye.)

Four Jews in a Room Bitching

(FOUR MEN—MARVIN, MENDEL, JASON, *and* WHIZZER—
*enter in darkness. Each carries a flashlight and wears
sunglasses.* WHIZZER *has a toy bed.*)

FOUR MEN:
Four Jews in a room bitching.
Four Jews in a room plot a crime.
I'm bitching. He's bitching.
They're bitching. We're bitching.
Bitch bitch bitch bitch
Funny funny funny funny

(*They point their flashlights at the bed and slowly
kneel.*)

Bitch—bitch—
Bitch bitch bitch bitch
All—the—
Time . . .

(TRINA *enters.*)

MENDEL:	OTHER MEN:
Whadda they do for love?	
	Ooooh.

(MENDEL *shines his flashlight at* TRINA'S
chest.)

Whadda they do for love?	
	Ooooh.

ALL:
Four Jews in a room

MENDEL:
Bitching

JASON:
Bitching

MARVIN:
Bitching

WHIZZER:
Bitching

FOUR MEN:
Four Jews in a room stoop—

MENDEL:
They stoop—

FOUR MEN:
—to pray.

JASON (*through door*):
I'm Jewish.

MARVIN (*through door*):
I'm Jewish.

MENDEL:
I'm Jewish.

WHIZZER (*through door*):
Half-Jewish.

FOUR MEN:
Bitch bitch bitch bitch
Funny funny funny funny
Bitch—bitch
Bitch bitch bitch bitch
Night and day.

(*The* MEN *run offstage.* TRINA *drags in a huge wooden representation of the Red Sea.*)

TRINA:
Slavery. Slavery.

FOUR MEN (*returning in biblical robes*):
We crossed the desert
Running for our lives
Fleeing from the Pharaoh
Who was up to no good.

Now we're at the Red Sea
Pharaoh is behind us
Wanting us extincted.

JASON:
What a we need's a miracle!

ALL:
And then the Red Sea
Split before us—

(*The Red Sea splits and flies offstage.*)

No more tsouris.

MENDEL:
We got our miracle!

JASON (*echoing*):
We got our miracle!

MARVIN (*another echo*):
We got our miracle!

ALL:
Four Jews itching for answers
Four Jews bitching their whole life long.

WHIZZER:
I'm Whizzer.

JASON:
I'm Jason.

MENDEL:
I'm Mendel.

MARVIN:
I'm Marvin.

FOUR MEN:
Bitch bitch bitch bitch
Funny funny funny funny
Bitch—bitch—
Bitch bitch bitch bitch
Right or wrong.

JASON:
In case of smoke please call our mothers on the phone
And say their sons are all on fire

MARVIN AND WHIZZER:
We are manipulating people and we need to know
Our worst sides aren't ignored.

MENDEL (*opens door and enters, arm gallantly in air*):
The guilt invested will, in time, pay wisely.

WHIZZER AND JASON:
We do not tippy-toe.

WHIZZER:
We charge ahead to show—

MENDEL:
We're good in bed.

(WHIZZER *puts his hand on* MENDEL'S *shoulder*).

WHIZZER:
Excel in bed.

(MARVIN *puts his hand on* WHIZZER'S *shoulder*.)

MARVIN:
We smell in bed.

(WHIZZER *puts his hand on* MARVIN'S. JASON *picks up the bed and hides it behind his back*.)

JASON:
Where is the bed?

MENDEL:
I love the bed.

JASON:
Who has the bed?

WHIZZER:
I want the bed.

(MENDEL *takes the bed from* JASON.)

JASON:
Who stole the bed?

MARVIN:
Who stole the bed?

WHIZZER:
I lost it twice.

(MENDEL *puts the bed on the floor.* ALL *go to floor, toward bed.*)

MENDEL:
The bed is mine.

WHIZZER:
The bed is nice.

FOUR MEN:
The bed is—
Four Jews in a room bitching (wheee!)
Four Jews talking like Jew-ish men
I'm neurotic, he's neurotic,
They're neurotic, we're neurotic.
Bitch bitch bitch bitch
Funny funny funny funny.

MARVIN:
I'm nauseous.

WHIZZER:
I'm nauseous.

JASON:
I'm simple.

MENDEL:
I'm Jewish.

TRINA (*vacuuming*):
Slavery. Slavery.

FOUR MEN (*at* TRINA):
Bitch bitch bitch bitch
Funny funny funny funny.

WHIZZER:
I'm neurotic, he's
  neurotic
They're neurotic,
  we're neurotic
Four Jews
In a room
Bitching
Bitch bitch bitch
  bitch

MENDEL:
Bitch bitch bitch
  bitch
Funny, funny,
  funny, funny
He's Jewish, I'm
  Jewish
They're Jewish,
  we're Jewish
Bitch bitch bitch
  bitch
Funny funny
  funny funny

MARVIN AND
JASON:
He's Jewish, I'm
  Jewish
They're Jewish,
  we're Jewish
Bitch bitch bitch
  bitch
Funny, funny,
  funny, funny
Four Jews
In a room
  bitching

FOUR MEN:
Four Jews in a room bitching

MARVIN:
In a room bitching

FOUR MEN:
Bitch—bitch—
Bitch bitch bitch bitch
Now and then.

Can't lose.
Loose screws.
Four—
One, two, three, four—

TRINA:
Five!

FOUR MEN:
Five Jews.

(*On button, the* MEN *make a Flying Wallenda finish.
Blackout.*)

A Tight-Knit Family

(*As the lights come up,* MENDEL *is in his office. Somewhere else,* MARVIN, *rumpled, sings.*)

MARVIN:
Well, the situation's this—
It's not tough to comprehend:
I divorced my wife,
I left my child
And I ran off with a friend.

But I want a tight-knit family.
I want a group that harmonizes.
I want my wife and kid and friend
To pretend
Time will mend
Our pain.

So the year is 'seventy-nine,
And we don't go by the book.
We all eat as one—

Wife, friend, and son.
And I sing out as they cook.

I love my tight-knit family.
I sing out: I love the way they cook linguine.
Isn't it great, we're all so swell.
Such a dear clientele.

I swear we're gonna come through it.
I fear we'll probably fight,
But nothing's impossible.
Live by your wit—
Kid, wife, and lover will have to admit
I was right.
I cushioned the fall.
I want it all.
I want it all.
I want it . . .
I want it . . . all.

(MARVIN *sits*.)

Love Is Blind

(TRINA *stands in the doorway of* MENDEL'S *office. He welcomes her in*.)

MENDEL:
Sit down, my dear,

(TRINA *sits*.)

I hear you have a problem.
I'm sure you're not disgusting or indiscreet—

(TRINA *looks at* MENDEL.)

Take a load off your feet.

(*He puts her feet on the ottoman.*)

Happy or sad?

(TRINA *starts to speak.*)

Don't.
That's a question with no answer.
Let's not discuss the weather; let's face the facts.
Marvin's wife must relax.

TRINA (*takes a breath and sings*):
Love isn't sex.
That's a thing my husband once told me.
Marvin, my ex—

(MARVIN *looks at* TRINA.)

You've seen him for years—
Told me over the phone to tell you my fears.
Do you only treat queers?

MENDEL:
Breathe deep, my dear—
You'll find me understanding.
Your pain is *a priori*;

(TRINA *takes off her sweater.*)

Unfold your untold story.
Now to break bread . . .
Loosen your glands;

(MENDEL *is leering.* TRINA *looks at him.*)

Put your head in my hands.

(TRINA *leans back.*)

TRINA:
I'm everything he wanted.
It's time I put it all together:
The date was set—
My father let me marry.
I married. I . . .

Then Marvin came from work.
Sat me down on the bed.
He told me how he loved me,
How he needed and/or valued me.
I have . . .

MENDEL:
What?

MARVIN (*as* TRINA *mouths*):
Syphilis.

TRINA:
He said.

MENDEL:
Good.

TRINA:
I have . . .

MENDEL:
Yes?

MARVIN (*as* TRINA *mouths*):
Syphilis.

TRINA:
It's true.

MENDEL:
Good.

TRINA:
I have something rotten
Which appeared
Though now it's well forgotten.

MARVIN:
Maybe, darling, so do you.

TRINA:
Maybe, darling, so do you.

(WHIZZER, *having just come from the gym, enters with
a gym bag containing a handball racquet.* JASON *slides*
TRINA, *sitting in a chair with wheels, back to* MARVIN.
She drops her scarf. MENDEL *picks it up and smells it.*
MARVIN *looks at* WHIZZER.)

I am probably diseased.

MENDEL:
You're a lovely girl.

TRINA (*laughing*):
And so easily appeased.

MENDEL:
What a lovely girl,

Though she's possibly diseased.
(*He puts the scarf away.*)

TRINA:
He took pains to not excite us.
He explains I've . . .

MARVIN (*as* TRINA *mouths*):
Hepatitis.

TRINA:
Too.

MARVIN, JASON, WHIZZER:
Hepa-, hepa-
Hepatitis
Hepatitis
Hepatitis.

(JASON *sits between* MARVIN *and* TRINA. WHIZZER
*takes two pictures, one of them with their glasses, one
without.* MENDEL *wipes his hands with a tissue.*)

MENDEL:
Love is blind.
Love can tell a million stories.
Love's unkind,
Spiteful in a million ways.

TRINA (*back in* MENDEL'*s office*):
Then I stayed home from work,
Took good care of my men.
They faked despair; they wet their bed.
They combed their hair; they acted dead.
One said . . .

MENDEL:
Yes?

JASON:
Daddy is a prick.

MENDEL:
What?

TRINA:
He said . . .

MENDEL:
Yes?

JASON:
Daddy isn't mine.

MENDEL:
Good

(WHIZZER *and* MARVIN *are talking upstage.* MARVIN *brings* JASON *over to meet* WHIZZER. JASON *shakes his hand then walks away.*)

TRINA:
He filled my coats with
Candies and notes, with
"Will you be my valentine?"

MARVIN (*to* WHIZZER):
Will you be my valentine?

TRINA:
This gets harder to believe.

MENDEL:
You're a damaged girl.

TRINA:
I've a scalpel up my sleeve.

MEN:
What a damaged girl.

MENDEL:
Do not ever slit your wrists.

TRINA:
I've missed him, he's still missing.

(MARVIN *and* WHIZZER *approach as if to kiss.*)

Don't make noise, but Daddy's kissing—
Boys.

MEN:
Petty, petty, petty, petty.

(TRINA *sits.*)

MENDEL AND TRINA:
Love is blind.
Love can tell a million stories.
Love's unkind,
Spiteful in a million ways.

ALL:
Love is blind.
Love can tell a million stories.
Love's unkind,
Spiteful in a million ways.

MARVIN:	OTHERS:
Love is crazy.	Love—
Love is often boring.	
Love stinks.	Love—
Love is pretty often debris.	
When you find	Love—
What you find,	
Then never, never, never, never, never	Love—
Do it over again.	
Love reads like a bad biography;	Love—
All the names are changed to protect the	Love—
innocent.	

ALL:
Love is blind.

(MENDEL *moves between* MARVIN *and* TRINA. *He is in the light. The* OTHERS *freeze.*)

MENDEL:
My name is Mendel.
I treat her husband—
I think she's very insecure.
But so am I.

I've never married.
Work . . . work is my passion.
Or perhaps that's an alibi.

MARVIN (*speaking*):
Perhaps it is.

MENDEL (*speaking*):
I don't care to discuss it.

(*Singing:*)
I think she's charming.
I think she's needy.
In just five sessions on my couch,
She'll be like new.

ALL (EXCEPT MENDEL):
His name is Mendel.

(*Everyone looks at* MENDEL. MENDEL *raises his arms.*)

WHIZZER:
Ah, ah.

MENDEL (*to* TRINA):
Return next Friday.

(TRINA *rises.* MENDEL *takes her hand.*)

I admit I admire you.

Thrill of First Love

(MARVIN *takes off his jacket and drops it on the floor. During the song,* WHIZZER *and* MARVIN *enjoy the competition. They fight and love it.*)

WHIZZER:
Pick up all your clothes.

MARVIN:
Whizzer begs.

WHIZZER:
Whizzer knows.

MARVIN:
Shave your legs.

WHIZZER:
Make me sick.

MARVIN:
You're a prick.

WHIZZER:
God, you're impossible.
We've been together for nine months.

MARVIN:
Ten months.

WHIZZER:
Nine months.

MARVIN:
Ten months.

WHIZZER:
Nine months.

MARVIN:
Ten months.
We are the salt of the bourgeoisie.

WHIZZER:
While I put the steak in . . .

MARVIN:
I bring home the bacon.

BOTH:
And we're proud to say we love it how we . . .

WHIZZER: MARVIN:
. . . won't . . .   . . . don't . . .
. . . won't . . .   . . . don't . . .

BOTH:
. . . agree.

WHIZZER:
Everything he owns is vile.

(*He reminds* MARVIN *of his jacket on the floor.*)

Marvin doesn't care a whit.
Marvin doesn't share my devotion to style.

(MARVIN *picks up his jacket.*)

Men from France can cancel a debt.
Men in cufflinks make me forget
My name.
I intend to upset
This regrettable game.

MARVIN:
Whizzer takes me by the neck.

WHIZZER:
Isn't that a French lapel?

MARVIN:
Whizzer has unlimited knowledge of dreck.

WHIZZER:
Send me flowers.

MARVIN:
Mention is made.

WHIZZER:
Make them roses.

MARVIN:
Attention is paid in full.

(MARVIN *again drops his jacket on the floor.*)

WHIZZER:
See how quickly he sours.

MARVIN:
When he pushes, I pull.

WHIZZER:
Pick up your clothes, Marvin.
Breeding shows, Marvin.

MARVIN:
I was rich,
He was horny.

WHIZZER:
We fit like a glove.

(MARVIN *puts his head on* WHIZZER'S *lap.*)

MARVIN:
Close your eyes, Whizzer.

WHIZZER:
Passion dies.
But I'd kill for that thrill of first love.

(WHIZZER *mock-chokes* MARVIN.)

BOTH:
We ask for passion at all times.
We stand to passion and drink this toast.

WHIZZER:
Still it's awfully trying . . .

MARVIN:
And we're not denying . . .

BOTH:
That of all the lesser passions.
We like fighting most.

MARVIN:
Whizzer screws too much to see

(WHIZZER *ties his shoes and straightens his socks.*)

What a joy is chastity,
What a joy is saving his joys
For one man.

WHIZZER:
Leave me.

MARVIN:
Love me.

WHIZZER:
Don't be a fool.

MARVIN:
Want me.

WHIZZER:
Feed me.

MARVIN:
No one's so cruel and cheap.

WHIZZER:
What I love, I devour.

MARVIN:
What you love, you devour.
What I covet, I keep.
Isn't that right, Whizzer?
Let's both fight, Whizzer.

WHIZZER:
I was trained in karate.

MARVIN:
I'm best when I cheat,

(MARVIN *puts his hand on* WHIZZER'S *shoulder, holding him down.*)

So I'll cheat, Whizzer, and I'll shove,
And I'd kill for that thrill of first love.

WHIZZER:
We've been together for nine months.

MARVIN:
Ten months.

WHIZZER:
Nine months.

MARVIN:
We've been together for ten months.

WHIZZER:
Nine months.

MARVIN:
Ten months.
In fact, we've almost survived a year.

WHIZZER:
True, but . . .

BOTH:
Who is counting?
We're too busy mounting
A display of our affection
That is so sincere.

(There's a thirty-measure interlude during which any-
thing can happen.)

BOTH:
Passion dies.
Passion dies.

WHIZZER:	MARVIN:
I would kill for that thrill	
Of first love.	I would kill for that thrill
I would kill for that thrill	Of first love.
Of first love	I would kill for that thrill

BOTH:
I would kill for that thrill of first

Love.
Love.
Lo——ve.

(*Blackout.*)

Marvin at the Psychiatrist

(JASON *is playing chess at home.*)

JASON:
My father says that love
Is the most beautiful thing in the world.
I think games are.
I think chess is the most
Beautiful thing.
Not love.

(WHIZZER *opens the door to* MENDEL'S *office and speaks.*)

WHIZZER:
Marvin at the Psychiatrist, a three-part mini-opera.
   Part one.

(*He closes the door.*)

MENDEL:
Do you love him?

MARVIN:
Sorta kinda.

MENDEL:
Do you need him?

MARVIN:
Sorta kinda.
He makes me smile a lot,
Especially at mealtime.
Makes me feel I'm
Sorta smart.

MENDEL:
Is he special?

MARVIN:
He's delightful.

MENDEL:
And romantic?

MARVIN:
Yes, and spiteful.
But then it seems that so am I.

MENDEL:
Just enjoy what you can—
Love the boy, not the man.

(MENDEL *"lays hands" on* MARVIN'S *head.*)

MARVIN (*echoing*):
Man.

(*He looks back to* WHIZZER.)

Sorta stylish.

MENDEL:
Kinda very.

MARVIN:
Very, very sorta.

MENDEL:
And kinda hard to describe.

MARVIN (*speaking*):
Oh, yes. Oh, I think that's very true.

MENDEL:
When he's naked . . .

MARVIN (*matter-of-fact*):
Yes.

MENDEL:
Does he thrill you?

MARVIN (*smiling*):
Yes.

MENDEL (*smiling*):
Is he vicious?

MARVIN:
Yes.

MENDEL:
Would he kill you?

MARVIN (*rueful*):
Yes.
I think he's sorta kinda mean.

But I love him
And I need it.
If he loved me,
I'd concede it.

MENDEL:
Don't despise what you feel.

(*He raises his arms for a laying on of hands.*)

Love the friend,
Not the heel.

MARVIN (*echoing*):
Heel.

(MENDEL *removes his hands, and* MARVIN's *head drops.*)

MENDEL:
He's sometimes worthless.

MARVIN:
Sometimes evil.

MENDEL:
Sometimes smarmy?

(MARVIN *turns to face* MENDEL.)

WHIZZER (*opening the door and speaking*):
Part two.

(*He closes the door. Part two is a new session.*)

MENDEL:
It's queer, Mr. Marvin.

(MARVIN *gives a look.*)

MARVIN (*speaking*):
Jesus.

MENDEL:
Sorry . . . *strange*, Mr. Marvin,
How your wife's—your ex-wife's—meager glories,
Coupled with her tragic stories,
Move me in unreported ways.

MARVIN:
She's a very good woman.
She's a wonderful woman.

MENDEL:
Do you mind that . . .
She was here to speak of Jason and I find that . . .
I hope Jason acts out more.
There's a few more things we need explore.

MARVIN (*speaking*):
She told me.

MENDEL (*speaking*):
Good.
I feel a lot better already. Okay. Going on.

(*He pats* MARVIN'S *shoulder. Singing:*)

Was she a vicious woman?

MARVIN:
No.

MENDEL:
Did she beat the child?

MARVIN:
No.

MENDEL (*more interested*):
Did she ever drive you wild?

MARVIN:
No.

MENDEL (*crestfallen*):
Never?

MARVIN:
No.

MENDEL:
Never?

MARVIN:
No.

MENDEL:
Never, never, never, never?

MARVIN:
No.

MENDEL:
Never?

MARVIN:
No.

MENDEL:
Never?

MARVIN (*upset, looking at* MENDEL):
No, no, no!

MENDEL:
Was she faithful?
Be objective.

MARVIN:
Yes.

MENDEL (*hopeful*):
She was faithful.

MARVIN:
Yes.

MENDEL:
And her last caress was . . .

(*He looks to* MARVIN *to finish the sentence.*)

MARVIN:
Careless.

MENDEL:
You mean "careful."

MARVIN:
Careful not to show she cared.

MENDEL:
So you weren't prepared

(*He rocks back and forth.*)

For the crying
And the screaming . . .

MARVIN (*more upset*):
And the beating of the breast.

MENDEL (*in orgasm, mouthing an audible*):
Aaaaaaaah!

(*Back in control.*)

I'm sorry.

MARVIN (*staring at him and speaking*):
What's wrong with you?
I mean, I don't mean to be rude.

MENDEL:
Does she sleep in the nude?

MARVIN (*speaking*):
No.

MENDEL (*unhappily, speaking as he writes in his notebook*):
Does not sleep nude.

(*Rips the page from his notebook and throws it out. Turns to* MARVIN, *speaking:*)

Okay. Going on.

(*Singing:*)

Did you like that?
Would she change it if she knew
You didn't like that?
Did she wear a negligee?
Could you blow and it would blow away?

(MENDEL, *is caught sniffing the scarf* TRINA *left behind earlier.*)

I don't mean to interfere.
I would like to make that very clear.

(MENDEL *tries to shake the scarf from his hand, but it won't fall.*)

WHIZZER (*opening the door and speaking*):
Part three.

(*He closes the door.*)

(MARVIN *is once more at the psychiatrist's.* JASON *is still at home with his chessboard.*)

MARVIN:
My son's distressing.

JASON:
My father's snide.

MARVIN:
I'm convalescing.

JASON:
He's morbid and dissatisfied.

MARVIN:
What should I do now?

JASON:
He loves another.

MARVIN:
I agree.

JASON:
I love my mother.

MARVIN:
Why not me?
We go to ball games.

JASON:
The ball is tossed.

MARVIN:
The pitcher's handsome.

JASON:
Yeah, and our team lost.

MARVIN:
Is that my problem?
Should I be blamed for that?

JASON:
Explore museums.

MARVIN:
Admire art.

JASON:
We stand together.

MARVIN:
But we stand there looking miles apart.
How do I reach him?
What words of wisdom?
What should I do now?

(JASON *stands, holding a king.*)

JASON:
My father says that love
Is the most beautiful thing in the world.
I think games are.
I think chess is the most
Beautiful thing,
Not love.

(JASON *sits.*)

MENDEL (*speaking*):
Marvin at the Psychiatrist, a three-part mini-opera.
   The end.

(*Fade to black.*)

My Father's a Homo

(*As the lights come up,* JASON *stands and sings.*)

JASON:
My father's a homo.
My mother's not thrilled at all.
Father homo . . .

What about chromo-somes?
Do they carry?
Will they carry?
Who's the homo now?

My father said that one day I'll grow up to be
     president,
And that idea's not so wild.
I don't lead the life of a normal child . . .

'Cause I'm too smart for my own good,
And I'm too good for my sorry little life.
My mother's no wife

(TRINA *enters.*)

And my father's no man,
No man at all.

Everyone Tells Jason to See a Psychiatrist

TRINA (*speaking*):
Honey, why don't you go out and play?

JASON (*speaking*):
No.

(*He begins to play chess with himself. Quickly playing
one side, turning the board, moving a piece, turning
the board again, moving, etc.*)

TRINA (*speaking*):
You want to go to the museum?

(JASON *shakes his head no.*)

TRINA:
Sweetheart, I worry.
Sweetheart, I do.
I worry a lot,
I worry a lot,
I worry a lot.

(*Speaking:*)

I could take you to the Jewish Center.

(*Singing:*)

I think you like playing chess alone.
That's not normal.

JASON:
What is normal?

TRINA (*speaking*):
I wouldn't know.

(*Singing:*)

Why don't you speak on the telephone
With anyone?
Just get a friend—anyone.
Darling, please see a psychiatrist.
He's quite a guy
And I admire how he acts.
No one is saying you're a sick neurotic,
But you could find some help.
Hear me out, please.
Yes, you could find some help.
He could help you re-a-lize
How confused you are.

It's very clear:
Daddy's sincere,
But a schmo.
You and I must trust our emotions,
Make no commotions.
Will you go?

JASON (*speaking*):
No.

MARVIN:
Jason, please see a psychiatrist.
He's just a psychiatrist.
I'll pay the bill
Until
You're old.

MARVIN:
Jason, please see
  a psychiatrist.
He's just a
  psychiatrist.
I'll pay the bill
Until
You're old.

TRINA:
Darling, please
  listen to your
  father here.
He's not a genius
  type, Lord
  knows,
But he knows
  what's true.
He chose a man
  who I think
  knows the
  answers
To all your
  problems.
Mendel under-
  stands what's
  bothering you.

JASON:
No, I won't go.
I will not go.
Never never
Never never
Never.

JASON (*speaking*):
Forget it.

ALL THREE (*grouped together as if for a photograph*):
What a mess this is,
This family.
Experts can see
This is so.

(*Photo flash; they all make faces like a parody of a
happy family portrait, then relax.*)

Photographs can't
Capture our magic,
We're simply tragic.

MARVIN AND TRINA:
Will you go?

(*They look at* JASON.)

JASON (*speaking*):
No.

(MARVIN *and* TRINA *rise and pull him by his shoulders and seat him on the ottoman.*)

MARVIN AND TRINA:
Jason, please see a psychiatrist.

(*They sit.*)

He's not—

JASON:
I won't say boo.

MARVIN AND TRINA:
—exorbitant,
And he's very smart.

JASON:
If intelligence were the only criterion,
Then I really wouldn't need a psychiatrist,

(*To* TRINA:)

Would I?

TRINA (*speaking*):
No.

JASON (*to* MARVIN, *speaking*):
Would I?

MARVIN (*speaking*):
No.

JASON (*speaking*):
Just because you've failed as parents.

(*Slight pause;* MARVIN *and* TRINA *stand.*)

TRINA (*outraged*):
Get thee to a psychiatrist.

MARVIN:
Hey, kid, listen.

JASON:
I don't need . . .

MARVIN AND TRINA (*to each other, still furious*):
He needs a psychiatrist.

JASON:
I want . . .

MARVIN AND TRINA:
A psychiatrist.

JASON:
I wanna speak with Whizzer.

MARVIN:
Speak with whom?

JASON:
With Whizzer.

MARVIN:
With Whizzer?

TRINA (*smiling*):
With Whizzer.

JASON:
With Whizzer.

MARVIN (*speaking*):
Oh, my God.

(MARVIN *and* TRINA *sit.*)

MARVIN, TRINA, JASON:
Whizzer.
Whizzer.

(*Doorbell.* WHIZZER *enters through the door, tapping his broken watch.*)

Whizzer.
Whizzer.

(WHIZZER *kneels between* MARVIN *and* JASON.)

JASON:
Whizzer, do you think I should see a psychiatrist?

WHIZZER:
I'm not sure, Jason.

(MARVIN *touches* WHIZZER'*s back.* WHIZZER *looks at him.*)

Oh—Jason, maybe so.

(TRINA *looks at* WHIZZER *over* JASON'*s head.*)

Absolutely, Jason.

(*They all await* JASON'*s response.*)

JASON:
Okay, I'll go.

WHIZZER:
He'll go.

JASON:
I'll go.

TRINA:
He'll go.

JASON:
If he comes here.

MARVIN:
If he comes here?

TRINA:
He might come here.

MARVIN:
They don't make house calls.

WHIZZER (*looking at his watch*):
Uh-oh.

This Had Better Come to a Stop

WHIZZER:
Late for dinner, late again.

WHIZZER, MARVIN, TRINA:
Late for dinner, late again.

ALL EXCEPT WHIZZER:
Late for dinner, late again.
Late for dinner—late, late, late, late.

(*During the following "Late for dinner" section,* TRINA
goes to the psychiatrist, JASON *to his chess set, and*
MARVIN *and* WHIZZER *fight at home.*)

Late for dinner, late again.
Late for dinner, late again.
Late for dinner, late again.
Late for dinner—late, late, late, late.

MARVIN (*to* WHIZZER):
Whizzer's supposed to always be here,
Making dinner, set to screw.
That's what pretty boys should do.
Check their hairlines, make the dinner,
And love me.

This is going nowhere but fast, Whizzer.
This little thing that we have will not last.
Don't feel responsible.
After all, it's through.

WHIZZER:
I'm not responsible.

MARVIN:
Life can be wonderful—
Isn't it wonderful?—and
This had better come to a stop, Whizzer.
Now, Whizzer . . .
Ciao, Whizzer.
Bend.

(WHIZZER *stands*.)

This had better come to an end.

TRINA (*at the psychiatrist's*):
I was supposed to make the dinner,
Make it pretty on his plate.
Every wife should pull her weight.
Have it ready, make it tasty
And love him.

This had better come to a stop, Doctor.
This has been a tragic and horrible flop.

MENDEL:
Don't feel responsible.
After all, it's through.

TRINA:
Who *is* responsible?

MENDEL:
Don't ask me questions.
I'm frightened of questions,
But grateful that it's
Come to a stop, Trina.
Smile, Trina.
I'll help you mend.

TRINA AND WHIZZER (*yelling at* MARVIN):
I met this man today.
He wasn't very smart.
But he was rich, Marvin.
Which, Marvin,
Do you prefer I lust for—
Brains or money?

MARVIN: MENDEL, TRINA, WHIZZER:
Brains. I'm not so rich,   Brains or money?
But hell, I'm smart.
Love me.

TRINA, WHIZZER, JASON, MENDEL (*speaking*):
No.

MARVIN:
Love me, please—
Or break my heart.

TRINA AND WHIZZER:
This is all
Very neat.
This is all
Very smart.

MARVIN:
This is all very neat.
This is all very neat.
This is all very smart.

MARVIN (*at the psychiatrist's*):
This had better come to a stop, Mendel.
Don't touch me.
Don't condescend.
This had better come—
This had better come to a—
This, this, this, this,
This had better come to an end.
This had better come to an end.

TRINA (*ranting against* MARVIN):
Chop chop chop chop chop.
I chopped it
And served his food.
The asshole forced me.

WHIZZER, MENDEL, JASON:
Chop chop chop chop
Chop chop chop chop.

TRINA:
And still the bastard divorced me.

(ALL *surround* MARVIN.)

TRINA (*loudest*):	MARVIN (*louder*):	OTHERS (*loud*):
		Chop chop chop chop
		Chop chop chop chop
	Late for dinner, late again.	Chop chop chop chop
It isn't like he says.	Late for dinner, late again.	Chop chop chop chop
You probably hurt his pride.	Late for dinner, late again.	Chop chop chop chop
He's gotta have it all.	Late for dinner, late again.	Chop chop chop chop
He's like a baby who's	Late for dinner, late again.	Chop chop chop chop
Denied.	Late for dinner, late again.	Chop chop chop chop

WHIZZER, MENDEL, JASON:
This had better come to a stop, Marvin.

ALL EXCEPT MARVIN:
This has been a lousy but fabulous flop.

WHIZZER:
Why is it always ourselves who have to change?

MARVIN (*speaking*):
This is incredibly boring.

WHIZZER AND TRINA:
You've got a temper that redefines temper and—

ALL EXCEPT MARVIN:
This had better come to a stop, Marvin.
Why, Marvin . . .
Try, Marvin.
Bend.

This had better come—
This had better come to a—
This this this this
This had better come
To an end.

MARVIN (*leaning forward*):
This had better come to an
end.

ALL:
This has better come to an end.

(*On the final "end,"* ALL *put their hands on* MARVIN'S
*shoulders, pull him back on musical button, and dis-
perse.* MARVIN *holds until lights are totally black.*)

I'm Breaking Down

(*The lights come up on* TRINA, *tying her apron.*)

TRINA:
I'd like to be a princess on a throne,
To have a country I can call my own.
And a king
Who's lusty and requires a fling
With a female thing.
Great . . . Men will be men . . .
Let me turn on the gas.
I saw them in the den
With Marvin grabbing Whizzer's ass.

Oh sure, I'm sure he's sure he did his best.
I mean, he tried to be what he was not.
The things he was are things which I've forgot.
He's a queen.
I'm a queen.
Where is our crown?

I'm breaking down
I'm breaking down.
My life is shitty
And my kid seems like an idiot to me.
I mean, that's wrong.
I mean, he's great.
It's me who is the matter,
Talking madder than the maddest hatter.
If I repeat one more word,
I swear I'll lose my brain.
What else should I explain?
Oh yes, it's true I can cry on cue
But so can you.
I'm breaking down.
I'm breaking down.
Down. Down.
You ask me, "Is it fun to cry over nothing?"
It is.
I'm breaking down.

(*Speaking:*)

Oh darn, don't have time for a breakdown now.
Have to get back to my banana-carrot surprise.

(*She cuts her finger while chopping.*)

Oh, that really hurt.

(*Singing:*)

Now let's consolidate our simple thoughts.
A healthy fruit is healthy till it rots.
I agree.
We sat beneath an apple tree.
Marv, his friend, and me.

Now, speaking of friends,
Whizzer is sweet and trim.
I think he sets the trends.
I think, in fact, I'll marry him.
He wants me!
I want to hate him, but I really can't.
It's like a nightmare how this all proceeds.
I hope that Whizzer don't fulfill his needs.
"Don't" is wrong.
Sing along.
What was the noun?

I'm breaking down.
I'm breaking down.
I'll soon redecorate these stalls.
I'd like some padding on the walls.
And also pills.
I wanna sleep.
Sure, things will prob'ly worsen,
But it's not like I'm some healthy person.
I've rethought my talks with Marv
And one fact does emerge:
I think I like his shrink.
So that is why I could use a drink.
I'm on the brink
Of breaking down.
I'm breaking down.
Down. Down.
I only want to love a man who can love me
Or like me
Or help me.

Marvin was never mine.
He took his meetings in the boys' latrine.
I used to cry.
He'd make a scene.

I'd rather die than dry clean
Marvin's wedding gown.
I'm breaking down.
I'm breaking down.
It's so upsetting when I found
That what's rectangular is round.
I mean, it stinks.
I mean, he's queer.
And me, I'm just a freak
Who needs it maybe every other week.
I've rethought the fun we had
And one fact does emerge:
I've played a foolish clown.
The almost-virgin who sings this dirge
Is on the verge of breaking down.
I'm breaking down.
Down. Down.
The only thing that's breaking *up*
Is my family.

The only thing that's breaking *up*
Is my family.
But me, I'm breaking down.
Down.

(*She collapses.*)

(*Blackout.*)

Please Come to My House

(TRINA *is on the phone.*)

TRINA:
Dr. Mendel, please.
Dr. Mendel, vis à vis what
    Marvin did,
Or rather, hasn't done,
You must exorcise a devil
'Cause it inhabits Marvin's
    son.

MENDEL (*speaking*):
Hello . . . Yes.

Trina, how are you?
(Uh huh.)

TRINA:
Please come to our house
And talk a bit to Jason.
It's a slight exaggeration,
But he's sick in the head.
Oh, sure,
Sometimes you'll think he's wonderful,
But he's wild.
I'm sure he's Marvin's child.

JASON (*to* TRINA):
What should I say to the man?
Should I be mean to the man?

TRINA:
Just be yourself.

JASON:
I'll be myself.

TRINA:
Stop asking questions. Be yourself.

JASON:
I'll be myself.

TRINA:
Don't be disgusting. Be yourself.

(*Doorbell.* MENDEL *opens the door.* MENDEL*and* JASON *shake hands.*)

JASON:
Hello to my house.
So good of you to travel.
On account of my unraveling.
Now let's eat some food.

MENDEL:
Let's talk.

TRINA:
I think before the food gets cold . . .

MENDEL:
Time to jaw.
First I'll extend my paw.

(*Ridiculously, chivalrously, he takes* TRINA'S *hand. Spotlight on their hands.*)

I think she's holding it so tenderly
I'll probably faint.
If so,
I'd rather die in this position
Than remain the saint
You think
You know.
I'm not,
Although
I must be showing better-than-the-norm restraint.

(*They all look at the dinner table.*)

ALL THREE:
Oh, what a lovely table.

(They are dancing with the table.)

Such a romantic table.
Knives in place,
Lotsa space
To spread out and eat.
Notice how our eyes discreetly . . .

(They look. Cat and mouse.)

ALL THREE *(in a round)*:
Please come to our house.
The dinner's on the table.
We will talk if we are able to,
But prob'ly we won't.
We sit.

MENDEL:
The kid looks pretty miserable.

(He puts an arm around JASON.*)*

JASON:
Uninspired.

MENDEL *(appreciating* JASON'S *attitude)*:
Ain't that the truth?

ALL THREE:
We're tired.

*(*JASON *moves* MENDEL'S *arm away.)*

MENDEL *(to* TRINA*)*:
I think the room looks just a wee bit small.

TRINA:
This girl agrees.

MENDEL AND JASON:
Adieu.

TRINA:
I'll wait outside.
Perhaps some food.

MENDEL:
I do not eat at all in times like these.

TRINA (*to* JASON):
The worst is through.

MENDEL:
There's work to do.

TRINA (*to* MENDEL):
I'll wait.

MENDEL (*looking at* TRINA, *then turning to the audience*):
She'll wait.

JASON (*between them*):
They'll wait.

TRINA:
I'll wait for you.

(TRINA *exits with the table.*)

Jason's Therapy

(JASON *is sitting;* MENDEL *paces.*)

JASON:
Mr. Mendel,
I get apoplexy thinking of my father.
I resemble him in far too many ways.
His sad demeanor,
The way he acts the swine;
At least his room is cleaner than mine.
Is it fatal?
Do you see real similarities between us?
He and Whizzer live like . . .
Well, I think it's clear.
Whaddo I do?
Whaddo I say?
How do I ask?
Whaddo I hope for?
Is it my mind?
Love isn't free.
Love isn't blind.
Whaddo I see?

MENDEL:
Stop.

(*He "lays hands" on* JASON'S *head.*)

Look around you.

(*He turns* JASON'S *head.*)

No one's screaming at you,
So you feel all right for ten minutes.
If you feel all right for ten minutes,

Why don't you feel all right for twenty minutes?
Feel all right for forty minutes?
Drop it and smile.

(*He scissor-jumps and shimmies.*)

Why don't you feel all right for the rest of your life?

(*Scissor jump.*)

Why don't you feel all right for the rest of your life?

(*Scissor jump.*)

Why don't you feel all right for the rest of your life?

(*He spins, halts.*)

JASON (*speaking to the audience*):
Is this therapy?

(TRINA *enters with a tableful of food.*)

TRINA:
Chop chop chop chop chop.
I chopped it.
It's a gourmet version of chicken merengo.
Took me all day.
I'll say 'twas worth the time.
I lie.

(MARVIN *enters.*)

MARVIN:
Why is he always here?

(MENDEL, *seeing* MARVIN, *runs off.*)

MARVIN, JASON, TRINA:
Five sessions later.

WHIZZER:
The psychiatrist returning,
Returning.

MENDEL (*entering through door*):
Try to forget all things homely.
Try to forget all things snide.
Nothing's as good as you recall.
Count what's good, then divide.

If you count, it's all right.
You can figure out the world.
You can add and subtract at will
You can cover up the past.
You can kill the pain
Very easily.

JASON:
Is this therapy?

ALL EXCEPT JASON:
Right, this is therapy.

JASON:
Oh!

JASON:
Mr. Mendel,

(JASON *sits* MENDEL *down.*)

As regarding your intentions to my mother.
Are they everything a woman would desire?

Her hand is ready.
It only needs a ring.
I'll buy confetti and sing.

(MENDEL *looks sheepish.*)

I'm embarrassed.
It's not my responsibility to ask you,
But I wonder if it's ever crossed your mind.

MENDEL (*to the audience*):
Whaddo I say?
Where do I look?
Why do I laugh?
How do I answer?
Is it my mind?
Love isn't free.
Love isn't blind.
Whaddo I see?

JASON:
Stop.

(*He lays his hands on* MENDEL'S *head.*)

Look around you.

(*He turns* MENDEL'S *head.*)

A lotta nice furniture.
Someone's bringing you dinner.
Someone brought you your lunch.
Someone's washing your laundry.
Washing your socks.
Jesus Christ!

(JASON *replicates* MENDEL'S *dance.*)

Why don't you feel all right for the rest of your life?

(*More dancing.*)

Why don't you feel all right for the rest of your life?

(*Still more dancing.*)

JASON AND MENDEL (*three scissor kicks, side by side*):
Why doncha [don't I] feel all right for the rest of
your [my] life?

(MARVIN *enters carrying a huge portrait of Freud.*)

ALL (MENDEL *sings "Why don't I . . . my life?"*):

Why doncha feel all right for the rest of your life?

(WHIZZER *enters carrying a huge portrait of Jung.*)

Why doncha feel all right for the rest of your life?

(TRINA *enters carrying a huge portrait of Dr. Ruth
Westheimer.*)

Why doncha feel all right for the rest of your life?

(*The band stands and sways. The mouths of the por-
traits start flapping in time to the music.*)

JASON AND MENDEL:	OTHERS:
Feel all right for the rest of your life	Feel feel feel
Feel all right for the rest of your life	Feel feel feel
Feel all right for the rest of your life	Feel feel feel

Feel all right for the rest of your life   Feel feel feel
Feel all right for the rest of your
Rest of your
LI-I-IFE!

(*Blackout.*)

A Marriage Proposal

JASON (*speaking to the audience*):
This is how you make a marriage proposal.

(*He starts to exit, then stops to indicate to* MENDEL
that he should propose. MARVIN *is sitting there watching the whole thing.*)

MENDEL:
I love you, dear.
I think you're swell.
You're never near me close enough to tell
If I'm delightful or not.
I crave your wrist.
I praise your thigh.
There's not a guy,
There's not a piece of paper,
There's not a man in pants
Who could love you the same as I.
Oftentimes lovers are crazy people.

(*He looks at* MARVIN.)

Sometimes they kill each other.
Just like a biblical brother
Did to his biblical brother
Back in biblical times.

TRINA, MARVIN, MENDEL (*speaking in succession*):
Biblical times . . .

MENDEL:
Oh, those biblical times!
I love your eyes.
I love your face.
I want you by my side
To take my place
If I get sick or detained.

(TRINA *laughs.*)

Don't touch your hair.
You're perfect.
Don't start to cry.
There's not a guy,
There's not a horse or zebra,
There's not a giant man,
Who could love you the same as I.
Forget that giant man.
He can't love you the same as I.
I'm not a giant man—

TRINA (*speaking*):
Good.

MENDEL (*crossing to* TRINA *and kneeling*):
—but I'll love you until
Love you until

(*He takes* TRINA'S *hand.*)

I die.

(*They kiss passionately.*)

A Tight-Knit Family (Reprise)

MARVIN:
Well, the situation's this:
I could use a little drink.
But I divorced my wife,
She dried her eyes,
Then she ran off with my shrink.

But I want a tight-knit family.
I want a wife who knows what love is.
Maybe she does.
I'm too damn peeved,
Self-absorbed,
Self-deceived.
Who knows?

MENDEL:
I should worry what he says,
Like his words could hurt me worse.
Marvin acts bereft.
My acts of theft
Are incredibly perverse.

MARVIN:
You said it.

MENDEL:
It's embarrassing, but
I've got a nice tight family:
Son with a brain and nice bright mother.
Yes, I feel guilt.
Yes, I'm annoyed.
So was Jung.
So was Freud.

MENDEL:
But I,
I know you'll come
   through it.
If so,
You'll end looking rich.

MARVIN:
I . . . I can't believe she
   loves you.
Why,
I'm sure she cannot love
   you.

MARVIN:
But nothing's impossible.

MENDEL:
Look who's got power.

MARVIN:
King of the losers.

MENDEL:
At eighty an hour
He can bitch, I can stall.

MARVIN:
I want . . .

MENDEL:
I got . . .

MARVIN:
I want . . .

BOTH:
. . . it all.
I'm sure we're gonna come through it.
No doubt the bastard prepares.
We're needy and wanting.
We're greedy as swine.

MENDEL:
I just bought a family.

MARVIN:
The fam'ly was mine.

BOTH:
But who dares
Dares to brawl.

MENDEL:
I got it all
I got it all
I got it all.

MARVIN:
I want it all
I want it all
I want it all.

(*Blackout.*)

Trina's Song

TRINA:
I'm tired of all the happy men who rule the world.
They grow—of that I'm sure.
They grow—but don't mature.
I'd like the chance to hide in that world.
I'm list'ning
As these men who aren't quite men yet, but aren't
    boys,
Make noise, and throw their knives;
Their toys are people's lives.
They fight too hard
And play too rough;
They sometimes love, but not enough.
My heart will beat at will, but still . . .

It's crazy how they're acting

And it's crazy my response.
And it's stupid how I love them,
So dumb how I anticipate their wants.
But as long as they amuse me,
That alone is what's required.
So I'll roar
Like I'm wired,
I'll explore what I'm feeling,
Except what I'm feeling
Is tired.
I'm tired,
So tired of all the happy men who rule the world.
Happy, frightened men who rule the world.
Stupid, charming men.
Silly, childish jerks.
That said, I'll be his wife.
I'll wed and change my life.
I'll laugh, I'll smile, I'll welcome cheer;
The time is right, the men are near.
Now happiness and love appear.

(*The four* MEN *march in, wearing gauze versions of
their costumes, with their sexual things either exposed
or exaggerated in neon. The effect should be both silly
and eerie.*)

March of the Falsettos

(*Everyone marches and everyone sings in falsetto.
Every so often everyone jumps together, and when they
do their voices get even higher. They're very serious
and very foolish and very manly.*)

MEN:
March. March.

March of the falsettos
March of the falsettos.
Who is
Man enough to march to
March of the falsettos?
One foot
Following the other.
Teach it to your brother.
Make him
March
March
March of the falsettos
March of the falsettos.

March a little bit
March a little bit
March a little bit
On.

Four men swaying
In phosphorescence,
Keep replaying
Their adolescence.

Four men marching
But never mincing,
Four men marching
Is so convincing.

MARVIN:
March.

MENDEL:
March.

JASON:
March.

WHIZZER:
March.

MENDEL:
Marvin's always wary.

MARVIN:
March.

MENDEL:
March.

JASON:
March.

WHIZZER:
March.

JASON:
Does this mean that I'm a fairy?

MARVIN:
March.

MENDEL:
March.

JASON:
March.

WHIZZER:
March.

MENDEL (*to* JASON):
What a stupid theory.

MARVIN:
March.

MENDEL:
March.

JASON:
March.

WHIZZER:
March.

WHIZZER (*to* JASON):
Whizzer says it doesn't, dearie.
Don't be scared,
Don't get tight.
Asses bared.
Such delight
Shared—

JASON:
With—

MARVIN:
Four—

WHIZZER:
Young—

MENDEL:
Men—

ALL FOUR:
Alone in the night.

(*They start a grotesque and hilarious soft-shoe.* MEN-
DEL *is twirling in circles.*)

ALL FOUR:
March. March.
March of the falsettos
March of the falsettos.

(*They turn.*)

Who is
Man enough to march to
March of the falsettos?

(*They patty-cake.*)

MARVIN, JASON:	MENDEL, WHIZZER:
One foot	One foot, oooh!
Following the other!	Following the other!
Practice it on one another.	Practice it on one another.
March. March.	March. March.

WHIZZER, JASON:
March of
   the falsettos
March of
   the falsettos
March of
   the falsettos
March of
   the falsettos.

MENDEL, MARVIN (*echoing*):

March of
   the falsettos
March of
   the falsettos
March of
   the falsettos
March of
   the falsettos.

ALL FOUR:
Marching
Home.

(*The "home" is sung very off-key. All four men back up. They wave on button.*)

(*Blackout.*)

Trina's Song (Reprise)

(*The lights come up on* TRINA. *She is dressed like Mendel.*)

TRINA:
Please forgive my former shpieling—
It does not concern the man.
As for doubts that I've been feeling,
I'll ignore them when I can.
And the things that I must do.
I'l do to make this all succeed.
I'll commit, that's agreed.
And with wit and precision
I've made a decision
To get the things I need,
God, I'll try, I'll try, I'll cry.

I'll laugh—and unafraid,
I'll laugh—then fire the maid.
I'll fight the gods, I'll fight my ex,
I'll beat the odds and have good sex.
My future's now on trial.
I smile.

The Chess Game

(MARVIN *and* WHIZZER *are playing chess.* MARVIN *is instructing* WHIZZER.)

MARVIN:
That's the king. Treat him nice.
Use some brains; now protect him.

WHIZZER:
Yes, I know. Here I go.

(*Pause;* WHIZZER *tries to decide what move to make.*)

MARVIN (*annoyed*):
Play the game.

WHIZZER:
Please don't watch me.
I can do it.

MARVIN:
Have a little scotch.

(WHIZZER moves, lets go. MARVIN *makes a face.*)

WHIZZER:
Shit. I blew it.
Maybe you could show me where . . .
I fear
I've lost my head.

MARVIN:
Do you want my help?

WHIZZER:
No, I don't.

I can think it through myself.

MARVIN:
Start again. We've seen the worst.

(MARVIN *resets the pieces.*)

WHIZZER:
I'll go first.

(*Pause.*)

MARVIN:
Move a pawn.

WHIZZER:
No, sir.

MARVIN:
Move.

WHIZZER:
Where?

MARVIN:
There.

WHIZZER:
Here?

MARVIN:
Move a pawn.

WHIZZER:
Who?

MARVIN:
Not the queen.

WHIZZER:
Who?

MARVIN:
Jesus.

BOTH (*turning to face the audience*):
Life's a sham and
Every move is wrong.
We've examined
Every move as we move along.

MARVIN:
Winning is everything to me.

WHIZZER:
Nothing is everything to me.

(*Both turn to face the game.*)

MARVIN:
Winning is everything to me.

WHIZZER:
Nothing is everything to me.
Except sex . . .

MARVIN (*speaking*):
Move the pawn.

WHIZZER (*speaking*):
. . . and money.

(WHIZZER *finally makes a move.*)

MARVIN:
Good first move.

WHIZZER:
Quite all right.
Take a turn.

MARVIN:
Thank you kindly.

WHIZZER:
Move the pawn.
Move the pawn.

(MARVIN *reaches for a knight; the music stops.* WHIZ-ZER *puts his hand on* MARVIN'S *king's bishop's pawn.*)

Take my hand.

(MARVIN *does.*)

Play the game.

(*They move the pawn one square.*)

MARVIN:
God, you're pretty.

WHIZZER (*taking his hand away*):
More's the pity,
Since you need a man . . .

MARVIN:
What?

WHIZZER:
. . . who's brainy.

MARVIN:
Or . . .

BOTH:
. . . Witty.

MARVIN (*speaking*):
Move.

WHIZZER:
What should I do now?

MARVIN:
Move.

WHIZZER:
Where?

MARVIN:
There?

WHIZZER (*moving king's bishop*):
How should I behave myself?
Maybe we should call it quits?

MARVIN:
This game shits.

(*Slight pause.*)

WHIZZER:
Let me win.

MARVIN:
Yes, sir.

(*They're playing a speed round.*)

WHIZZER:
Please.

MARVIN:
Yes.

WHIZZER:
Thanks.

(*Things are getting out of hand.*)

MARVIN:
Wait!

(*More out of hand.*)

WHIZZER:
Whizzer wins.

MARVIN:
Wait!

WHIZZER:
Whizzer wins.

MARVIN:
Wait!

WHIZZER:
Checkmate.

BOTH (*swiveling to face the audience*):
Life's a sham and every move is wrong.
We've examined every move as we move along.

(MARVIN, *in a rage, throws all the furniture at* WHIZ-
ZER: *ottoman, sofa, door carom like domestic bumper
cars. As the furniture comes screaming at him,* WHIZ-
ZER *doesn't flinch.* MARVIN *gets* WHIZZER'S *suitcase
and slams it down at his feet.*)

WHIZZER:
Whizzer's supposed to make the dinner,
Be a patsy, lose at chess,
Always bravely acquiesce.
Clip the coupons, make the dinner . . .
And love him.

(*He rises.*)

This has gotta come to a stop, Marvin.

MARVIN (*echoing*):
This has gotta come to a stop, Whizzer.

WHIZZER:
This has been a lousy but

BOTH:
Fabulous flop.

MARVIN:
Anyone understand?
All I want's a kiss.
Anyone understand?

WHIZZER:
Don't start explaining. I'm sick of explaining.

BOTH:
And this had better come to a stop, Marvin [Whizzer].
Now, Marvin, [Whizzer].
Ciao, Marvin [Whizzer].
Bend.
This had better come—
This had better come to a—
This this this this

WHIZZER: MARVIN:
This had better
Come to an end.   This had better come to an end.

(WHIZZER *picks up the suitcase.*)

BOTH:
This had better come to an end.

(*Blackout.*)

Making a Home

(TRINA *enters through the door;* MENDEL *is close behind her, carrying a lighted menorah. This is the only
light in the room.* WHIZZER *opens his suitcase on a
table and starts packing.* MARVIN *exits through the
door.*)

MENDEL AND TRINA:
Welcome to our humble place

(MENDEL *puts the menorah on the table.*)

We're concerned with setting a tone
With filling the space,

(TRINA *sets the board for a game of chess.*)

Making a home.

(MENDEL *starts rearranging the furniture* MARVIN *threw at* WHIZZER. *It's their furniture now.*)

MENDEL:
She becomes a happy wife.

(*He begins to decide how to arrange the room; then he starts moving the modular units.*)

TRINA:
He decides the role to assume.
Building a life,

MENDEL:
Shaping a room.

MENDEL AND TRINA:
What it needs is people,
Men and women talking.
Men and women thinking out loud
How far to go.

Visit when you please—
You are not required to phone.
We'll buy the cheese.
God bless our home.

(*Light floods in.* TRINA *sits in a chair and sings to the*

audience while MENDEL *renovates.* JASON *hands* TRINA
a dog leash like he's afraid to touch it.)

TRINA:
Books abound
To show we read.
The dog's been flea'd
And sent outside to play.
I hope it runs away.

MENDEL:
So do I.

JASON:
So do I.

MENDEL AND TRINA:
Afternoons we make hors d'oeuvres.
After afternoons we receive.

WHIZZER:
We deceive.

MENDEL AND TRINA:
This is the price.

WHIZZER:
This is the price.

MENDEL, TRINA, WHIZZER:
Making believe.

What it needs is people.
Men and women laughing.
Men and women thinking out loud.

TRINA: MENDEL: WHIZZER:
Should he
  love me?   Should she
          love me?   Could he love me?

MENDEL, TRINA:
Yes, we love the bed.
Yes, we love to fight the unknown.

TRINA:
Baking the bread.

MENDEL:
Sharpening knives.

MENDEL, TRINA, WHIZZER:
Forging ahead.

MENDEL:
Loving our—

TRINA:
Liking our—

WHIZZER AND JASON:
Hating our—

ALL FOUR:
—lives.

MENDEL AND TRINA: WHIZZER:
Making a
  home.
Making a   Making a
  home.   home.
                Making a home.

MENDEL AND TRINA:
Making a home.

(JASON *sits down between* TRINA *and* MENDEL. WHIZ-
ZER *closes his suitcase and sings.*)

The Games I Play

WHIZZER:
I don't look for trouble,
I do not accept blame.
I've a good and a bad side,
But they're one and the same.
Ask me to arouse you,
I will rise and obey.
These are the games I play.

I screw every morning,
Then bathe and drink tea.
I've been playing canasta
Disasta-
Rously.
All my recreation seems to suit me okay.
These are the games I play.

It's tough with love,
Love's tough to show.
Let me face the music.
It's a song that I was
Waiting to hear so long
So long ago.

I bet on the horses.
I die by degree.
I am sure his divorce is

A tribute to me.
Ask me if I love him,
It depends on the day.
These are the games I play.

It's tough, my friend,
Love's looking strong.
Play again the music.
It's a song that I've been waiting to hear
For much too long.
Years,
Years too long.

It hurts not to love him.
It hurts when love fades.
It's hard when part of him
Is off playing fam'ly charades.
Ask me if I need him.
Get him out of my way:
These are
These are the games
These are the games
These are the only games
I play.

(WHIZZER *sits.* ALL *nervously await* MARVIN . . . *and then hell breaks loose.*)

Marvin Hits Trina

MARVIN:
Hello, Trina. Thank you for coming here.
Goodness, Trina, I am relieved.
Frankly, Trina, nice of you coming here.
Thank you, Trina.

I have received
Your new-sent wedding invitations.
They are—

MEN:
Pseudo-romantic and sick.

MARVIN:
You say you'll—

MEN:
Love him until you both die.

MARVIN:
You die on—

MEN:
May twenty-seventh at eight.

(MARVIN *has lost it. He's pulling the furniture out
from under* TRINA.)

WHIZZER (*swiveling to the audience*):
He has lost his mind.
Marvin is not so uncouth.
Marvin is not so unkind.

TRINA:
Mendel plans to rub my back.
Mendel's not a maniac.

(JASON *looks at* TRINA.)

And he's sweet

(TRINA *looks at* MARVIN.)

And he's warm
And he loves me so.

MARVIN:
Tell me, Trina, what was the impetus?
Sorry, Trina, look in my eyes.

(*He's glaring over her.*)

Really, Trina, this is ridiculous.
Jesus, Trina, how I despise

(*He backs* TRINA *into the table.*)

Your need for stupid conversation.
You are—

MEN:
Trying to ruin my sleep.

MARVIN:
I'm sure you—

MEN:
Chose him to make me look bad.

MARVIN:
How could you—

MEN:
Ever deny what we had?

WHIZZER (*in falsetto*) AND TRINA:
We had fights and games.
Marvin called us funny names.
Marvin always played the clown.

MENDEL (*Looking at* MARVIN *as* JASON *looks at*
MENDEL):
Marvin acts like he's untrained.
Marvin, I am so ashamed.

WHIZZER (*in falsetto*) AND TRINA:
And he's sweet. And he's mean.

WHIZZER:
Do I love him?

(*Considers.*)

No.

MARVIN:
I am so dumb.

THE OTHERS: MARVIN:
Dumb. Dumb.
Dumb. Dumb.   Why?

WHIZZER, MENDEL, MARVIN:
Whack!

(MARVIN *slaps* TRINA'S *face.* JASON *stares at* MARVIN.
*All is totally still until the music for "I Never Wanted
to Love You" begins.*)

I Never Wanted to Love You

TRINA (*holding her face*):
I never wanted to love you.
I only wanted to love and not be blamed.
Let me go.

You should know
I'm not ashamed
To have loved you.

MENDEL (*crossing to* TRINA):
I love you more than I meant to.
In my profession one's love stays unexpressed.
Here we stand.
Take my hand.
God, I'm distressed.
How I love you.

JASON:
I hate the world.

TRINA:
He hates everything.

JASON:
I love my dad.

WHIZZER:
He loves his father.

JASON:
I love the things I've never had.

TRINA AND MARVIN:
Love our family.

JASON:
Lord, hear our call.

MENDEL:
Help us all.

TRINA AND WHIZZER:
Help us all.

MARVIN, AND JASON:
Help us all.

MENDEL:
Help us all.

TRINA AND MARVIN:
Help us all.

WHIZZER (*to* MARVIN):
I never wanted to love you.
I never wanted "till death do we two part."
Condescend.
Stay my friend.
How do I start not to love you?

TRINA (*to the tune of* "Love Is Blind"):
I'm everything he wanted.
It's time I put it all together.
My hands were tied.
My father cried: "You'll marry!"
I married.

MARVIN (*to* JASON): I never wanted to love you. I only wanted to see my face in yours.	TRINA, JASON: He's mine.
(*To the audience:*)	
Jason smiled. Save this child. How he adores And hates me.	He's mine.

(*To* TRINA:)

It really killed me
When you took those vows.
Don't misunderstand
I'm in demand,
And anyhow, we're through.
I never wanted
I wanted
I never never never never
Never never wanted to love you.
I never wanted to love you.
I never wanted to   TRINA, WHIZZER, JASON:
Lo—ve
You   Lo—ve
Love you.   You.

(*Everyone exits but* JASON *and* MARVIN. JASON *moves
to his chessboard.* MARVIN *stands looking at him.*)

Father to Son

JASON:
My father says that love
Is the most beautiful thing in the world.
I think girls are.

(*On "girls," he pushes the chess table away from him.*)

I think girls are the most
Beautiful thing,
Not love.

MARVIN:
Kid, be my son.
What I've done to you is rotten.
Say, I was scared.
I kept marching in one place.
Marching in time to a tune I'd forgotten.
I loved you. I love you.
I meant no disgrace.
This here is love
When we're talking face to face.

(MARVIN *sits knee to knee with* JASON.)

Father to son,
I for one would take love slower.
I've made my choice.
But you can sing a different song.
Watch, as you sing,
How your voice gets much lower.
You'll be, kid, a man, kid—
If nothing goes wrong.
Sing for yourself
As you march along.

A man, kid, you'll be, kid—
Whatever your song.
Sing for us all
As we march along.

(JASON *puts out his hand to shake.* MARVIN *stands, lifts* JASON *to his feet, and, on the final note of the song,* JASON *throws his arms around* MARVIN.)

(*Fade to black.*)

Falsettoland

For Arthur Salvadore

"Falsettoland" opened at Playwrights Horizons, under the artistic direction of Andre Bishop, on June 28, 1990. The cast was as follows:

Marvin	Michael Rupert
Trina	Faith Prince
Jason	Danny Gerard
Whizzer	Stephen Bogardus
Mendel	Chip Zien
Dr. Charlotte	Heather MacRae
Cordelia	Janet Metz

It subsequently moved to the elegant, newly restored Lucille Lortel Theatre on September 16, 1990. It was produced by Maurice Rosenfield and Lois F. Rosenfield, Inc., with Steven Suskin in association with Playwrights Horizons and by special arrangement with Lucille Lortel. It was directed by James Lapine. The set was designed by Douglas Stein; the costumes were by Franne Lee, the lighting by Nancy Schertler, and the sound by Scott Lehrer. The musical direction and arrangements were by Michael Starobin. The stage manager was Kate Riddle.

(When the audience enters, they see a huge, three-dimensional "1981" on stage. Two huge flashlights—the kind used to land planes at airports—are seen at the back of the stage behind the numbers. We cannot see who is manipulating them, but the lights are slowly prescribing the dimensions of the stage. Then the flashlights are turned into the eyes of the audience.)

Opening

MENDEL (*acting as our tour guide*):
Homosexuals.

(*He searches the audience for them.*)

Women with children.

(*Ditto.*)

Short insomniacs.

(*He shines the lights on his face.*)

And a teeny tiny band.

(*He shines them on the band upstage. The band area lights up and the band waves.*)

Come back in,
The welcome mat is on the floor.
Let's begin.
This story needs an ending

(MARVIN *enters.*)

Homosexual.

(*Light on* MARVIN.)

Father with children.

(JASON *enters.*)

One bar mitzvah that
Is scrupulously planned.

(WHIZZER *and* TRINA *enter, followed by everyone else.*)

ALL:
Lovers come and lovers go.
Lovers fight and sing fortissimo.
Give these handsome boys a hand.
Welcome to Falsetto—

MEN:	DR. CHARLOTTE:	TRINA AND CORDELIA:
—land!	Nancy Reagan—	Ooooh.
	WOMEN:	

	Meanest and
	     thinnest of the
	     First Ladies—
	Moves into the
	     White House.	

MEN:
Yabba dabba
        It's the eighties.

ALL:
Yabba dabba

WOMEN:
Oooh the eighties.

MEN:
Yabba dabba

ALL:
What a world we live—

WOMEN:
In!

MEN:
March. March.
March of the falsettos.
March of the falsettos.

WOMEN:
What a world we live in!
Oooh
Wa-oooh!

MEN:

Who is
Man enough to march to
March of the falsettos?

ALL (*clapping*):
Yabba dabba dabba.

WOMEN:
Screwy families.

DR. CHARLOTTE:
Women internists.

CORDELIA:
Kosher caterers—

ALL:
Who are trying to expand.
Everybody on your mark.

WOMEN:
Congregate in Central Park.

MEN:
Pretty boys are in demand.

ALL:
Welcome to Falsettoland.
Heey!

(*Ingenious scissor-kick formations.*)

Hooo!

(*Great joyous havoc.*)

What a world we live in!

(MARVIN *looks around, perplexed.*)

Heey!

(*They're wheeling around on furniture.*)

Hooo!

(*Setting the scene.*)

What a world we live in!

(*Creating the world.*)

Heey!

(*The last scissor kick.*)

MARVIN (*looking disdainfully at them all*):
It's about time, don't you think?
It's about time to grow up,
Don't you think?
It's about time to grow up
And face the music.
It's about time.

(*To the audience:*)

Since we last spoke
Two years are waning.
I'll try explaining
Just what you've missed.

(TRINA *moves to his side.*)

We called a truce
And fitfully we coexist.

(MENDEL *moves to his side.*)

I'm still loose.
She's still with the psychiatrist.

(*They both walk away.*)

So I don't have a psychiatrist
Except on the Jewish holidays.
But I still have my son on the weekends,

(MARVIN *embraces* JASON.)

Just on the weekends,

(JASON *removes* MARVIN'*s arm and walks away.*)

And some very good friends.

(*The* LESBIANS, *on either side of him, kiss his cheek.*)

But I don't have a lover anymore.
Oh my God.
When am I going to get over this?
When am I going to get over this?
When am I going to get over this?

WHIZZER, CORDELIA, DR. CHARLOTTE:
Homosexuals.

TRINA AND JASON:
Women with children.

MARVIN, TRINA, WHIZZER:
Ex-ex-lovers.

MENDEL:
And a teeny tiny band.

ALL:
Welcome to Falsettoland.

MENDEL:
Psychoanalysts.

JASON:
Child insomniacs.

ALL:
Welcome to Falsettoland.
Liberal democrats.

CORDELIA AND DR. CHARLOTTE:
Spiky lesbians.

ALL:
Welcome to Falsettoland.

CORDELIA:
Kosher caterers.

    add MENDEL AND JASON:
    Short insomniacs.

    add DR. CHARLOTTE:
    Hypochondriacs.

    add MARVIN:
    Yiddish Americans.

    add WHIZZER:
    Screwy families.

    add TRINA:
    Radiologists.

ALL:
Intellectuals.
Nervous wrecks.
Ugh. Ah!
Welcome to Falsettoland.

(ALL *but* MARVIN *leave singing through the door Marvin has opened.*)

MARVIN:
It's about time, don't you think?
It's about time to grow up,
Don't you think?
It's about time to grow up
And face the music.
It's about time.

One day I'd like to be
As mature as my son,
Who is twelve and a half
And this tall

(*His hand indicates* JASON-*height.* JASON *slides in, right under his hand.*)

That's all I'd like to be, that's all.
It's about growing up,
Getting older,
Living on a lover's shoulder,
Learning love is not a crime.
It's about time.
It's about time.
It's about time.
It's about . . .

The Year of the Child

JASON (*listening to a Walkman and singing along*):
Baruch
Baruch atoh
Baruch atoh adonai
Baruch atoh adonai elohenu
Meluch haolum . . .

TRINA:
Jason, dear, hello.
Are you packed and waiting?
But before we go,
Let me speak with Father alone.

(*To* MARVIN:)

Now as this bar mitzvah nears—
Jason, put your Walkerman on and hum—

(*To* MARVIN:)

Since this is the last loving thing
We'll probably ever do together,
Let's act adult and not go crazy.

MARVIN:
Have you chosen yet who'll cater?

TRINA:
What about it?

MARVIN:
I know a person who should cater.

TRINA:
It's a personal opinion who should cater.

MARVIN:
Can we consider who's gonna cater?

TRINA:
Shh.

MARVIN:
Please.

TRINA:
Shh.

MARVIN:
Please.

TRINA:
Shh.

MARVIN:
Please.

MENDEL:
Stop!
This is so much crap.
Throw a simple party.
Religion's just a trap
That ensnares the weak and the dumb.
Stop with the prayers.

TRINA:
How can you stop with the prayers
At a bar mitzvah?

MENDEL:
The whole thing's voodoo,
And I know more than you do.

MARVIN AND TRINA:
This is the year of Jason's bar mitzvah.

MARVIN: TRINA:
We're more excited
Than we should be.   We're more excited
We're more ex—   Than we should be.

BOTH:
This is the year of the child
When he spreads out his wings.

There's music in his heart,
His life's about to start—
His body's going wild.

(JASON *is twitching to the Walkman.*)

My child.

MARVIN:
My child.

TRINA:
Our child.

MENDEL:
Children, please,
Throw the kid a celebration and relax.
I'll bring women
From the wrong side of the tracks.
We'll have a ball.
I guess I'll have to raise this Jason myself.

TRINA:	MARVIN:	MENDEL:
	Isn't he an asshole?	My own bar mitzvah was
Yes he is.	Isn't he too much?	A miserable occasion,
Yes, but so are you.	Jesus,	The cause for such abrasion
Really, kiddo,	What an asshole!	In my family.
So are you.	Jason, where's my hug?	It still gives me
Where's my hug?	Where's my—	hives.

MARVIN AND TRINA: MENDEL:
This is the year
   for Jason's bar mitzvah.   This is the year for Jason's
This is the year   bar mitzvah.
   for Jason's bar mitzvah.   This is the year for Jason's
                                   bar mitzvah.

(*Doorbell. Enter the* LESBIANS.)

DR. CHARLOTTE (*in the doorway*):
Look look look look look—
It's a lesbian from next door.

CORDELIA (*carrying a tray of food*):
Followed by her lover,
Who's a lesbian from next door too.
And I've got food for you,
Delicious food for you,
Nouvelle bar mitzvah cuisine.

TRINA:
Oh!

CORDELIA:
Here's dietetic knishes,
Gefilte fishes.
Food that's from the heart.
So take a bite and see
If all your friends agree
It's good.

ALL:
Yummy, yummy, yummy, yummy
Yummy, yummy, yummy, yummy
Yummy, yummy, yummy, yummy, yum.

We'll have one perfect time.
We'll spend billions of dollars.

MENDEL:
Conga!

ALL (*in a joyous, almost psychedelic conga line*):
We'll have flowers galore. Whoo!
And the band will sound fine. Whoo!
There'll be chandeliers set round the room,
With the men in tuxedoes.

(MARVIN *exits with the chair* JASON *is sitting on.*)

There'll be food like food never before.
What a day to remember!
This is the year,
   is the year,
      is the year of Jason's bar mitzvah.

JASON:
They're more excited than they should be.

(MARVIN *returns with a chair on which the word
"Jason" is written in Hebrew-like lettering.*)

ALL:
This is the year of the child,
When he spreads out his wings.
There's music in his heart.
His life's about to start
His body's going wild
My—

JASON AND MARVIN:
Chi-ild.

CORDELIA:
Chi-ild.

TRINA:
Chi-ild.

DR. CHARLOTTE AND MENDEL:
Chi-ild.

(*A Flying Wallenda finish.*)

Miracle of Judaism

(*Lights come up on* JASON, *leaning on a bat, wearing a "Jewish Center" T-shirt.*)

JASON:
Dot Nardoni.
Tiffany Axelrod.
Zoe Feinstein.
Angelina Dellibovi.
Bunny Doyne.
Or what's her name?
Mo Christafaro.
Or Heather Levin.
Brittany Rosenthal.
Which?
Flo Giu . . . Giu . . .
What is the name of that bitch?

(*He remembers.*)

Oh—Flo Giuseppe.
Right, but it borders on kitsch.

(JASON *swings a baseball bat.*)

Of these girls,
Which should I invite to my bar mitzvah?
I've a problem to flaunt:
I don't want the girls I should want.

VOICE (*of the piano player*):
Batter up!

(*Bleachers are pushed on stage, and our friends,*
TRINA, MENDEL, MARVIN, CORDELIA, *and* DR. CHAR-
LOTTE *sit down on them. Crowd noise as they watch
the baseball game.*)

JASON:
I want girls for whom I lust.
Girls who wear a lot of makeup.
Girls who smoke and show their bust.
Girls with whom I always wake up.

(*He takes a lousy swing.*)

VOICE:
Strike one!   (*Reaction from bleacher group.*)

JASON:
Would they come, though,
If they were invited?
And not
Laugh at my Hebrew?
And not
Laugh at my father and his friends?

VOICE:
Strike two!   (JASON *takes another awkward*
                        swing.)

JASON:
Excluding them I find exciting
And I'm left with them I'll be inviting.
Selecting girls for one's bar mitzvah—
God, that's the miracle of Judaism.

VOICE:
Strike three! You're out!

JASON (*walking away*):
That'd be the miracle of Judaism.

(*Consolation and cheer from bleacher group.*)

The Baseball Game

MARVIN, MENDEL, TRINA, CORDELIA, DR. CHARLOTTE
(*sitting together on the bleachers*):
We're sitting
And watching Jason play baseball.
We're watching Jason play baseball.
We're watching Jewish boys
Who cannot play baseball
Play baseball.
We're watching Jewish boys
Who cannot play baseball
Play . . .

MARVIN:
I hate baseball.
I really do.
Unlike the rest of you.
I hate baseball.

CORDELIA AND DR. CHARLOTTE (*about* MARVIN):
We really wish he'd take this more seriously.

MENDEL:
Ach, I like how he swings the bat.

MARVIN:
It's good how he swings the bat.
But why does he have to throw like that?

ALL THE SPECTATORS:
We're sitting
And watching Jason make errors.
The most pathetical errors.
We're watching Jewish boys
Who almost read Latin
Up battin'
And battin' bad.

MENDEL (*getting carried away*):
Remember Sandy Koufax.
You can do it
If you wanna do it.
Take heart from Hank Greenberg.
It's not genetic.
Anything can be copasetic.
I think
I think
I think it can.
I think it can.

ALL THE SPECTATORS:
We're sitting
And watching Jason play baseball.
We're watching Jason play baseball.
We're watching Jewish boys
We're watching Jewish boys
We're watching—
Slide, Jason—slide Jason, slide!

(WHIZZER *has entered*.)

MARVIN:
What is he doing here?

TRINA:
What are you doing here?

WHIZZER:
Jason asked me to come.
Since he asked me to come, I came.

TRINA:
Just what I wanted at a Little League game—
My ex-husband's ex-lover.
Isn't that what every mother
Dreams about having
At a Little League game?

MENDEL:
Looking at Whizzer is like
Eating *trayf*.

CORDELIA (*yelling at the umpire*):
The kid was out!

DR. CHARLOTTE (*yelling at the umpire*):
The kid was safe!

CORDELIA (*to* DR. CHARLOTTE):
The kid was out.

DR. CHARLOTTE (*to the umpire*):
The kid was safe!

WHIZZER (*answering* MARVIN'S *question*):
Hey, I love baseball.
I love baseball.
That's what I'm doing here.

DR. CHARLOTTE (*speaking, disgusted*):
Where the hell did they
Get that umpire?
Oh, hi, Whizzer.

MARVIN:
Look who's here.
Say hello.

WHIZZER (*speaking*):
Hello.

MARVIN:
You're looking sweeter than a donut.

WHIZZER (*shaking hands*):
Marvin.

MARVIN:
Whizzer.

WHIZZER (*to* TRINA):
He still queer?

MARVIN (*overhearing*):
Am I queer?

TRINA:
I don't know.

MENDEL:
Does it matter?

MARVIN:
It's been so long since I could tell.

(*To* WHIZZER:)

Sit in front of me.
I wanna see the bald spot.
C'mon, c'mon, move in front of me.
It gives me pleasure to see the bald spot.
Since it's the only physical imperfection that you've
   got,
I wanna see it.
I wanna touch it.
I wanna run my hands through it.

ALL:
We're sitting and watch the kid as he misses.
We're watching Marvin throw kisses.
We're watching sixty-seven pounders,
Watching Jewish boys miss grounders.
Watching boys field, boys bat,
Boys this, boys that.
Watching Jason on deck
Swinging the bat.

WHIZZER (*speaking*):
Hey, Jason.

JASON (*speaking*):
Oh, hi, Whizzer.

WHIZZER (*to* JASON*):*
Keep your head in the box,
Don't think of a thing.
Keep your head in the box,
Your eye on the ball,
Take a breath,
Then let it out and swing.

(WHIZZER *swings, beautifully.*)

MENDEL, CORDELIA, DR. CHARLOTTE:
Oooh.

WHIZZER:	OTHER SPECTATORS:
Keep your head in the box.	Keep your head in the box.
Don't think of a thing.	Don't think of a thing.
Keep your head in the box,	Keep your head in the box,
Your eye on the ball,	Your eye on the ball,

ALL THE SPECTATORS:
Take a breath,
Then let it out and swing.

WHIZZER (*speaking*):
Go get 'em.

(JASON *runs off.*)

MARVIN (*about* WHIZZER):
Even bald he looks good.

WHIZZER (*about* MARVIN):
Just remember he's psychotic.

MARVIN (*about* WHIZZER):
He looks damn good
But he's cheap as dirt.

WHIZZER:
Even maniacs can charm—
Which he does,
So beware.

MARVIN:
And just be careful.

WHIZZER:
When he smiles that smile, avoid him,
Or else sound the alert.

MARVIN (*speaking*):
Whizzer.

WHIZZER (*speaking*):
Marvin.

MARVIN (*speaking*):
So you think there's hope for the kid?

WHIZZER (*speaking*):
I love Jason, but this is not his venue.

BOTH:
How could I know

Without him
My life would be
Boring as shit?

MARVIN:
But it is . . .

WHIZZER (*yelling*):
Jason, move closer to the plate!

MARVIN:
Yes, it is . . .

(*He punches* WHIZZER *for suggesting that.*)

He's gonna be hit by the ball!

(WHIZZER *punches* MARVIN *back. They rub their arms.*)

BOTH:
Please, God, don't let me make the same mistake.

(*A ball rockets in.*)

MENDEL (*yelling*):
Heads up!

(MENDEL *catches it.*)

ALL THE SPECTATORS:
We're sitting and watching Jason the batter.
We know our cheering won't matter.
It is the very final inning
And the other team is winning.
And there's two outs, two strikes,
But the bases are loaded, and—

MARVIN (*to* WHIZZER *on the other side of the*
bleachers):
Would it be possible to see you
Or to kiss you
Or to give you a call?

ALL THE SPECTATORS (*on their feet, celebrating*):
Anything's possible.
Jason hit the ball!

(*They sit.* JASON, *never having hit a ball before, is still*
at home plate.)

Run!

A Day in Falsettoland

WHIZZER (*speaking*):
A day in Falsettoland.
Dr. Mendel at work.

PATIENT (*speaking*):
You go out on the street and there are all these people
asking for a handout. Then you go home and open your
mail, and it's full of people asking for donations. Then
you turn on your TV and they want money for starv-
ing children in Ethiopia.

MENDEL (*speaking*):
How does that make you feel?

PATIENT (*speaking*):
I mean, I just want to be left alone . . .

MENDEL:
I don't get it.
I don't understand.
In the sixties,
Everyone had heart.
In the sixties,
We were all a part
Of the same team.
In the sixties,
We had a new world to start.
Could this—
Oh God, don't say it is—
Could this be the new world we started?
There I sit brokenhearted.
And . . .

PATIENT (*speaking*):
Do I wait for the promotion, or do I take the IBM job?

MENDEL (*speaking*):
Well, uh, Diane—

PATIENT (*speaking*):
Caroline!

MENDEL (*frantically looking through his notes*):
Caroline?

(*She cries hysterically.*)

PATIENT:
Yes, Caroline!

MENDEL:
I don't get it.
I've been left behind.

Half my patients:
Yuppie pagans.
Modeled on the
Ronald Reagans.
Now the world is too pathetic
And I don't get it at all.

PATIENT (*speaking*):
I'm in a deep quandary about my career. What do you
think I should do?

MENDEL:
Time's up!

PATIENT:
Oh!

(*In another part of the stage,* TRINA *is stretching, preparing for a jog.*)

MENDEL:
At least there's Trina at home.
Trina in bed.
Trina obsessing
And sort of caressing
My head with her feet.
I once thought it was sweet
But I don't anymore.
Now I just snore.
'Cause I'm so exhausted
Listening as these yuppie farts complain,
Listening as their shallow hearts explain
Their lives.

DR. CHARLOTTE (*speaking*):
Trina works it out.

TRINA (*warming up*):
Marvin's back with Whizzer.
Just like how it was.
If I don't like Whizzer,
It's because my ex
Sure does.
Why should that upset me?
Sometimes I'm a lout.
Mendel serenades and Jason calms me.
Why should I be wilting
When their precious love
Is not in doubt?
Work it out!

JASON (*speaking*):
The neighbors relax after work.

CORDELIA (*shaking a martini*):
How was your day at the hospital?

DR. CHARLOTTE:
Unbelievable.
What is that smell?

CORDELIA:
Nouvelle bar mitzvah cuisine.
I've been practicing
Cuisine, bar mitzvah nouvelle.

(*She hands the* DOCTOR *some food.* MENDEL *approaches* TRINA, *sneakers in hand.*)

MENDEL (*speaking*):
Hi, honey.

CORDELIA (*asking if she likes it or not*):
Well?

TRINA (*as* MENDEL *kisses her*):
Hi, honey.

MENDEL:
How was your day?

TRINA:
It was terrible.
Did you hear that
Marvin's back with Whizzer?
Marvin's back with Whizzer.

MENDEL:
Drop it, sweetheart.
Give it up.
You know I love you.
What's the matter,
Trina darling?
I don't get it.
Why can't you let go?

TRINA:
Maybe in a mile I'll be okay.
I'll be happy when we finally have this bar mitzvah.

MENDEL:
Isn't it enough
I want you every night?

TRINA:
Ha!

MENDEL:
Every other night.

TRINA:
I wish.

MENDEL:
Every third night.

TRINA:
Hm.

MENDEL:
Drop it!
Everything will be all right.

(MENDEL *bumps her ass with his ass.*)

TRINA:
Everything will be all right.

(*They're panting even* before *the run.*)

BOTH:
Everything will be all right.

(*They run off.* CORDELIA *has just poured* DR. CHAR-
LOTTE *a martini.*)

CORDELIA:
How was your day
At the hospital?

DR. CHARLOTTE:
It was wonderful.
For the first time in months
Nobody died.

(*She raises her glass in celebration.*)

There were just
Heart attacks and gallstones;
Light bulbs up the ass;
Fake appendicitis which was gas,
Which I diagnosed;
People overdosed and I saved them.
I saved young people, old people,
One priest and one high-school principal.
Saving lives I feel invincible.
Yes I do.
Do you know how great my life is?
Do you know how great my life is?
Saving lives and loving you.

CORDELIA:
You save lives
And I save chicken fat.
I can't fucking deal with that.

DR. CHARLOTTE:
Do you know how great my life is?

CORDELIA:
Yes, I know how great your life is.

DR. CHARLOTTE:
Do you know how great
my life is?

MENDEL AND TRINA
(jogging):
Everything will be all
right.

CORDELIA:
Yes, I know how great your life is.

DR. CHARLOTTE:
Do you know how great
my life is?

MENDEL AND TRINA:
Everything will be all
right.

CORDELIA:
Yes, I know how great—

DR. CHARLOTTE:
Saving lives

BOTH:
And loving you.

MENDEL AND TRINA:
Everything will be all
right.

Racquetball

(WHIZZER, *all in white, looking great.* MARVIN, *in
baggy and colorful jams, looking baggy. No ball is
used; rather, when they make a shot, the racquet
scrapes the floor and sounds like a ball ricocheting off
a racquet. In the course of the scene,* WHIZZER *deci-
mates* MARVIN, *as you would expect.*)

WHIZZER:
It bounced twice.

MARVIN:
No it didn't.

WHIZZER:
Once, then twice.
You know it did.

MARVIN:
That's not nice.

WHIZZER:
No it isn't,
But you're a pain in the ass.

MARVIN:
You're a beast,
But at least
When you play me you win.

WHIZZER (*serving*):
You give up.

(MARVIN *tries to race the ball down but can't.*)

MARVIN:
I perspire.

WHIZZER (*serving*):
Where's the heat?
Where's the fire?

(MARVIN *tries to hit, to no avail.*)

Used to be you'd desire a fight.
So fight.

MARVIN:
So play.

(WHIZZER *doesn't move an inch; he's in total control.*
MARVIN *is killing himself, trying to get his racquet on
the ball.*)

WHIZZER:
One—two—three—four.

MARVIN:
One—two—three—four.

WHIZZER:
One—two—three—four.

MARVIN:
One—two—three—four.

WHIZZER:
One—two—three—four.

MARVIN:
One—two—three—four.

WHIZZER:
One—two—three—four.

MARVIN:
One—two—three—four.

(*Finally, by mistake,* MARVIN *hits a good shot.*)

WHIZZER:
Lucky dink.

MARVIN:
I'm finessing.

WHIZZER:
Something stinks in how you play.

MARVIN:
Don't you think it's a blessing
I'm so pathetically bad.

WHIZZER:
Just stay back.
Serve with force.
I'll attack
And, of course,
I will win.
Just give in to bliss.
And kiss . . .

MARVIN:
Let's go.
Do you know?
All I want is you.
Anything you do
Is all right.
Yes, it's all right.
Do you know?
All I want is you.

WHIZZER:
Hit your shoe.

MARVIN:
No it didn't.

WHIZZER:
Yes it did.
The game is through.

MARVIN:
That's not nice.

WHIZZER:
No it isn't.

MARVIN:
God, you're a pain in the ass.

WHIZZER:
Play it raw.
Don't play pretty.
Sex and games in New York City
Have gotta be played with flair
And passion,
With passion and flair.

WHIZZER (*speaking*):

Down the alley
High lob
Low drive
Ceiling shot
Into the corner
Four walls
Dink.

MARVIN AND WHIZZER:	CHARLOTTE:	TRINA AND MENDEL:
Do you know?	Do you know	
All I want is you.	How great my life is?	Everything will
	CORDELIA:	
	Everything will be all right.	
	CHARLOTTE:	
Anything you do.	Do you know	Be all right.
Is all right.	How great my life is?	Everything will
	CORDELIA:	
	Everything will be all right.	
	CHARLOTTE:	
Yes, it's all right.	Saving lives	Be all right.
	BOTH:	
	and loving you.	
Everything will	Everything will	Everything will
Everything will	Be all right.	Be all right.
Everything will	Everything will	Everything will
Everything will	Everything will	Be
Feel all right		We'll
For the rest of your life.	Everything will	Feel feel feel feel
	Be all right.	We're gonna be
Feel all right	Everything will	Feel feel feel feel
For the rest of your life.	Be all right.	We're gonna be
	Everything	Feel feel feel feel
Feel all right	will—	We're gonna
For the rest of your—		be—
Rest of your—		

JASON (*speaking*):
You people are so white.

ALL EXCEPT JASON:
Everything will be all right!

(*Blackout.*)

The Fight

JASON (*with a knapsack on his back*):
Just look at me:
I'm a world-class traveler.
Each Friday night
Travel travel travel
From her house to his house.
First take the 104
With my computer.
I'm just a little kid,
Not a commuter.
And each Sunday night
Mother comes to get me
And I hear them fight.
Everybody's yelling about the bar mitzvah.
It's not a wrestling match.
Why are they sweating?
It's not a funeral.
What's so upsetting?
It's a celebration
Where I get presents.
But everybody's yelling
And everybody's ruining it.
It's a celebration
Where I get richer.
But everybody's yelling
And everybody's ruining it.
Everybody's ruining it.
Why oh why,

What have I done that
They'd ruin my bar mitzvah?

	THE OTHERS:
What have I done that	What have we done that
They'd ruin my bar	We'd ruin his bar mitzvah?
mitzvah?	

TRINA:
I want the Applebaums.
They're lovely, and they like me.

MARVIN:
They're boring, and they like the way you dress.

MENDEL:
Well, who wouldn't?

TRINA:
Have the Applebaums.

MARVIN:
Screw the Applebaums.

JASON:
Please don't do this.

MARVIN:
He's no jerk.

TRINA:
Have them.

MARVIN:
Nix them.

MENDEL:
Long live the Applebaums!

Arguing takes work!

JASON:
I hate this.

MARVIN:
Blame her.
It is all a waste.

TRINA:
Look at your couch, it is homo-baroque.
Don't talk to me about taste.

JASON:
Stop! I don't want a bar mitzvah!
Okay! I don't want a bar mitzvah!

MARVIN AND TRINA (*quietly, sweetly*):
Whaddya mean you don't want a bar mitzvah?
Whaddya mean you don't want a bar mitzvah?
How do you think we
How do you think we
How do you think we feel about that?

(*Their faces are right in* JASON'*s.* MENDEL *sticks his
face between* TRINA'*s and* MARVIN'*s and scoots them
out of the room.*)

Everyone Hates His Parents

MENDEL:
Jason,
I am agitato grande.
Jason, I am muy disgutante
And muy disappointe

And muy nauseatus
And me mitzraim
Hotzionoo
Dayenu.
Oh—
Day, dayenu.
Day, dayenu.
Day, dayenu . . .

(*To* JASON)

Everyone hates his parents.
Don't be ashamed.
You'll grow up,
You'll come through,
You'll have kids
And they'll hate you too.
Oh, everyone hates his parents,
But I confess,
You grow up,
You get old,
You hate less.

JASON:
Still I don't want it.
Nothing that gives them pleasure
I'll do.
I don't want a bar mitzvah,
Stupid bar mitzvah,
Any bar mitzvah,
Would you?

MENDEL (*sliding* JASON *onto his knee*):
Everyone hates his parents
That's in the Torah.
It's what history shows.

In fact, God said to Moses:
"Moses, everyone hates his parents.
That's how it is."
And God knew
Because God hated his.

(MARVIN *re-enters and pulls* JASON *aside.*)

MARVIN (*trying desperately to sound reasonable*):
You are gonna kill your mother.
Don't feel guilty,
Kill your mother.
Rather than humiliate her,
Killing your mother is the merciful thing to do.

(TRINA *enters.*)

TRINA (*trying to calm herself*):
Jason, darling, don't get nervous.
I'm right here and at your service.
Look, I'm calm and self-deluded.
Grateful 'cause I hope you'll do
What I pray you'll do.

MARVIN:
Go ahead and kill your mother.

TRINA:
Not with guns, but kill your mother.

MARVIN AND TRINA:
Rather than humiliate her,
Killing your mother is the merciful thing to do.

(JASON *is fed up. He tries to hide by pulling his shirt*

over his head so that only a very squeezed face is visible in the neck hole.)

MENDEL:
Everyone hates his parents.
Now I see why.
But in time
They'll cool out
And you'll think
They were only fooling.
It's a strange thing about parents:
Push turns to shove—
What was hate
Becomes more or less love.

MARVIN AND TRINA:
Jason, please see a psychiatrist.

MENDEL (*speaking*):
I'm a psychiatrist. Get lost.

(MENDEL *pulls his shirt over his head and sings.*)

Everyone hates his parents.
This too shall pass.
You'll grow up.

JASON:
I'll come through.
I'll have kids.

MENDEL:
And they'll hate you too.

MENDEL AND JASON (*dancing*):
Oh, everyone hates his parents.

MENDEL:
But, kid, I guess
You'll grow up.

JASON:
I'll grow up.

MENDEL:
You'll get old.

JASON:
I'll get old.

JASON AND MENDEL:
And hate less.

(*They dance a great dance.*)

And hate less.
Yes!

(*They high-five.*)

(*Blackout.*)

What More Can I Say?

(*The lights rise on* MARVIN *and* WHIZZER *in bed. Slats of morning light cover the designer sheets. Above their heads is a Mapplethorpe of a calla lily.* MARVIN *is wearing a white T-shirt;* WHIZZER *is wearing nothing. During the whole song,* MARVIN *barely moves.* WHIZZER, *sleeping, is slowly moving—next to* MARVIN *or apart, into* MARVIN's *arms, onto his stomach or his back. Whatever, it's both hot and incredibly innocent.*)

MARVIN:
It's been hot,
Also very sweet.
And I'm not usually indiscreet.
But when he sparkles,
The earth begins to sway.
What more can I say?
How can I express
How confused am I by our happiness?
I can't eat breakfast,
I cannot tie my shoe.
What more can I do?

If I said I love him,
You might think my words come cheap.
Let's just say
I'm glad he's mine awake,
Asleep.

It's been hot
Also it's been swell.
More than not,
It's been more than words can tell.
I halt.
I stammer.
I sing a rondelay.
What more can I say?

I'll stay calm.
Untie my tongue.
And try to stay
Both kind and young.

I was taught
Never brag or shout.
Still it's hot,
Just like how you read about.

And also funny,
And never too uncouth.
That's the simple truth.

(WHIZZER *is sleeping face up.* MARVIN *looks underneath the sheet and is stunned by his good fortune.*)

Can you tell
I have been revised?
It's so swell,
Damn it, even I'm surprised.
We laugh,
We fumble,
We take it day by day.
What more can I say?

(*Blackout.*)

Something Bad Is Happening

(*On one side of the stage,* DR. CHARLOTTE *is reading a medical journal; on the other,* CORDELIA *is devising recipes from a cookbook,* New Jewish Recipes.)

DR. CHARLOTTE:
People might think
I'm very dykish.
I make a big stink
When I must—but god damn;
I'm just professional,
Never too nonchalant.
If I'm a bitch—
Well, I am what I am.

Just call me Doc.
Don't call me Lady.
I don't like to talk
When I'm losing the game.
Bachelors arrive sick and frightened.
They leave weeks later, unenlightened.
We see a trend, but the trend has no name.

(*She holds up the journal.*)

Something bad is happening.
Something very bad is happening.
Something stinks,
Something immoral,
Something so bad that words
Have lost their meaning.
Rumors fly and tales abound.
Stories echo underground.
Something bad is spreading
Spreading
Spreading round.

(CORDELIA *gives* DR. CHARLOTTE *some food.*)

CORDELIA:
Tell me how it tastes.
Tell me if it's good.
Tell me, dear, if you'd like seconds.

DR. CHARLOTTE:
Stop!

CORDELIA:
Go ahead and wound my pride.

DR. CHARLOTTE:
Just stop!

CORDELIA:
You're feeling very sick inside.
I can tell.
And it's something I cooked.
I just knew how you looked.

(*To the audience*:)

Look what I've done to my doctor.

(DR. CHARLOTTE *cannot believe she is hearing this.*
She picks up and reads a copy of Interview *magazine.*)

She's my doctor, and I love her.
She's got passion.
She's intelligent, and, Jesus Christ,
A doctor. Very wealthy.
And I love her.
Doctor of Internal Medicine.
I'm sorry that you're queasy.

DR. CHARLOTTE:
I'm uneasy.

CORDELIA:
She's got something on her mind
That makes her nervous.

DR. CHARLOTTE:
This is fucking ridiculous.

CORDELIA:
She's my doctor, and I love her.
She's got—

DR. CHARLOTTE:
I scan the mag.
Very chic tabloid—
The men dressed in drag
Next to their moms.
Fashion and passion and
    filler
But not a word about the
    killer.
I like the ball gowns,
But Jesus Christ!
Something bad is
    happening.
Something very bad is
    happening
Something stinks.

Something immoral,
Something so bad that
    words
Have lost their meaning.
Rumors fly and tales
    abound.
Stories echo underground.
Something bad is—

CORDELIA:
Heart!

Something bad is
    happening.

Look, I made her sick.

She ate the food and she
    got sick.
Oh, woe is me.
Oh, woe is me.

BOTH:
Spreading
Spreading
Spreading round.

DR. CHARLOTTE:
Look, a virus has been found.
Stories echo underground.
Something bad is—

BOTH:
Spreading
Spreading
Spreading round.

Second Racquetball

(MARVIN *is winning when the game is called.*)

WHIZZER (*winded*):
It bounced in.

MARVIN:
No it didn't.

WHIZZER:
Hit the line—
You know it did.

MARVIN:
Just begin.

WHIZZER:
Are you kidding?
Who's telling who how to play?

MARVIN:
Let me live,
Please forgive me for winning one game.

WHIZZER:
Serve it up.

MARVIN:
I attack.

WHIZZER (*on the defensive*):
Hold him down,
Keep it back,
Something's gone out of whack.

MARVIN (*a great shot*):
I hit—

WHIZZER (*sprawling on the floor*):
Aw, shit.

MARVIN:
My game.

(*Serving:*)

One—two—three—four.

WHIZZER (*missing the ball;* MARVIN *is very pleased*):

One—two—three—
Damn it.

MARVIN (*serving*):
One—two—three—four.

WHIZZER:
One—two—

(*He can't get the serve.*)

Good serve, Marvin.

MARVIN:
One—two—three—four.

(WHIZZER *blows the shot, trips over his own feet.*)

WHIZZER:
One—
Hit my heel.

MARVIN:
Don't be bitter.

WHIZZER (*walking off the court*):
No big deal.
The game is yours.

MARVIN:
It's unreal,
You're a quitter.

WHIZZER:
I can't go on anymore.

MARVIN:
Be a jerk,
My sweet bruiser.
Try to be a decent loser.
At least you could give me that.

(*Disgustedly*, MARVIN *throws his racquet toward*
WHIZZER.)

WHIZZER:
Excuse me, I'm ready to go.
I'm ready to . . .

(WHIZZER *goes to pick up the racquet and almost collapses.* MARVIN *rushes to hold him up.*)

MARVIN:
Do you know
All I want is you?
Anything you do
Is all right.

(WHIZZER *tries to walk away but can't. He stands,
bent over, trying to catch his breath.*)

MARVIN (*holding* WHIZZER *up*):	THE OTHERS EXCEPT WHIZZER:
Yes, it's all right.	Everything will be all right.
Yes, it is.	Everything will be all right.
	Everything will be all right.

Holding to the Ground

(*As* MARVIN *and* WHIZZER *slowly make their way upstage,* TRINA *draws a white curtain across the stage.
We see* TRINA *look at* MARVIN, *who looks scared to
death; and then* WHIZZER *sitting on a hospital bed,
being examined by* DR. CHARLOTTE. TRINA *fleetingly
sees* MENDEL; *she sees* MARVIN; *voices are singing "Everything will be all right."* TRINA *turns to the
audience.*)

TRINA:
I was sure growing up I would live the life
My mother assumed I'd live.
Very Jewish.
Very middle class.

And very straight.
Where healthy men
Stayed healthy men
And marriages were long and great.

I smile.
I don't complain.
I'm trying to keep sane as the rules keep changing.
Families aren't what they were.
Thank God there's a husband and a child whom I
    adore.
But then there's more.
So many more.
There's always more.
Life is never what you planned
Life is moments you can't understand.
And that is life.

I'm plain.
I don't astound.
I hold to the ground as the ground keeps shifting,
Keeping my balance square.
Trying not to care about this man who Marvin loves.
But that's my life.
He shared my life.
Yes, that's my life.
Life is never what you planned.
Life is moments you can't understand.
And that is life.

(*The curtain is opened on* WHIZZER, *white as a ghost,
lying in a hospital bed.*)

Holding to the ground as the ground keeps shifting.
Trying to keep sane as the rules keep changing.
Keeping up my head as my heart falls out of sight.

Everything will be all right.
Everything will be all . . .

(She can't finish and walks out.)

Days Like This I Almost Believe in God

(MARVIN enters the hospital room with great, hearty enthusiasm. He is obviously petrified.)

MARVIN:
Whizzer,
Kid, you're looking very good today.
You had to see yourself a few days back.
I had a heart attack.
Jesus.
But today you seem to be
On the way to recovery.
Oh, Whizzer, I want to applaud.
It's days like this I almost believe in God.
Days like this I almost believe in God.

(CORDELIA enters with a tray of Jewish stuff.)

MARVIN AND WHIZZER *(speaking)*:
Hello.

CORDELIA *(speaking)*:
Hello.

(Displaying the tray for WHIZZER, she sings:)

Rugelach. Gefilte fish.
It's so good you'd think it's Italian.
Also a soup made from chicken

That, though unexotic,
Is antibiotic.
Oh, I'm up to my ass
In a kosher morass.
For aches and croup, try my chicken soup.

(*They start the descant.*)

MARVIN:
Whizzer,
Kid, you're looking
Very good today.
You had to see yourself a
  few days back.
I had a heart attack.
Jesus.
But . . .

CORDELIA:
So let's begin. It's
  medicine.
It could be we're both
  going to cure you.
Me with my soup,
She with her medication.
Such elation.
But . . .

MARVIN AND CORDELIA:
Today
You seem to be
On the way to recovery.
Oh, Whizzer, I want to applaud.
It's days like this
We almost believe in God.
Days like this we almost believe in—

CORDELIA:
Gefilte fish.

MARVIN:
God.

CORDELIA:
Canadelach.

(TRINA *walks in with a plant.* MENDEL *follows.*)

TRINA:
Hi.
He had trouble parking.
Just like on our second date.

MENDEL:
I hyperventilate.
But since I'm parking in the city,
I've improved.
Or else the hydrants moved.

(*Only* CORDELIA *laughs.*)

Yeah, go ahead,
Be good and pissed.
"How can I help?" says the wiry psychiatrist.

TRINA:
He'll make you well.

WHIZZER (*speaking*):
Right.

MENDEL:
I'll make you well.

(JASON *enters with a chessboard.* DR. CHARLOTTE
follows.)

JASON AND DR. CHARLOTTE:
Whizzer, hello.

(DR. CHARLOTTE *hugs* CORDELIA.)

JASON (*going to the bed*):
Gee, you look awful.
I think you need to play some chess.

WHIZZER:
Jason, sit down and begin.

JASON:
I'll let you win, Whizzer.
I'll let you win.
I'll let you . . .

MARVIN AND CHARLOTTE:	CORDELIA:	MENDEL AND TRINA:	JASON:
Whizzer,	Rugelach.	I'll make you well.	Win.
Kid, you're looking very Good today.	Gefilte fish.	He'll make you	Whizzer hello.
You had to See yourself a	It's so good you'd Think it's Italian.	Well. I'll make you Well. He'll make you	Gee, you look aw—
Few days back. I had a Heart attack	Also a soup made From chicken that though	Well. I'll make you Well. He'll make you	Ful.
Jesus.	Unexotic, is Antibiotic.	Well. I'll make you Well.	I think you need to play some chess.

ALL EXCEPT WHIZZER:
But today you seem to be
On the way to recovery.
Oh, Whizzer, I want to applaud.
It's days like this we almost believe in God.
Days like this we almost believe in God.
Days like this we almost believe in God.
Days like this we almost believe in—

WHIZZER:
Sshhh!

TRINA: (*speaking*):
What is this?

CORDELIA:
Gefilte fish.

MENDEL:
I'll make you well.

MARVIN:
Right.

TRINA:
You're looking very good today.

CORDELIA:
Canadelach.

(*Everyone tastes* CORDELIA's *food.*)

ALL (*speaking*):
Ugh.

(*Singing:*)

God!

Canceling the Bar Mitzvah

TRINA:
Jason, if you want a bar mitzvah
God knows you can have a bar mitzvah.
But I have to know
And I have to know now
Just what it is you want.
I've addressed the invitations;
Here's your chance to give me hell.
If you think it's bust,
It is probably just
As well.

JASON:
Can't we wait till Whizzer gets better?
Can't we wait till he's out?
That's what bar mitzvahs should be all about.
Good friends close at hand—
Don't you understand?

(*Long pause. Music plays.*)

MENDEL:
We can't be sure when
He'll get better,
When or if
He'll ever get better.
But the hall is booked
And the band's been retained.
So Jason, please,
What we'll do is your decision.
There's no right and there's no wrong.
Just say yes or no
And we'll promise to go along.

JASON:
Finally now it's all my decision.
Like it's my bar mitzvah.
Just like nothing's happened.
Hell, let's have a party,
Just like nothing's happened.
Why don't you make this dumb decision yourselves,
Okay?
Why don't you make this dumb decision yourselves?

(JASON *moves upstage with his back to the audience.*)

MENDEL:
We'll have the bar mitzvah.

JASON (*speaking*):
No.

TRINA:
Then we'll cancel the bar mitzvah.

JASON (*speaking*):
No.

(JASON *storms out.*)

MENDEL AND TRINA (*as* JASON *storms out, still in control*):
We'll wait until you make a decision.

MENDEL (*speaking*):
I think that went well.

TRINA (*singing*):
Holding to the ground as the ground keeps shifting.

MENDEL:
Trying to keep sane as the rules keep changing.

BOTH:
Keeping up my head as my heart falls out of sight.
Everything will be all right.

Unlikely Lovers

(*In the hospital room,* MARVIN *is fussing with the bed.
In bed,* WHIZZER *plays solitaire and seems content.*)

MARVIN:
Who'd believe
That we two
Would end up as lovers?

WHIZZER:
Do you want me to reply?

MARVIN (*to the audience*):
Him and me.

(*To* WHIZZER:)

You and I.
Passionately lovers.

WHIZZER:
Please don't get morbid.

MARVIN:
Right.

WHIZZER:
It's just—

MARVIN:
Don't fight.

WHIZZER:
—that I haven't died yet.

MARVIN:
Just stop it.

WHIZZER:
I'm sick but kicking.

MARVIN:
Geez . . .

WHIZZER:
All right.

MARVIN:
Louise!

WHIZZER:
Good night.

MARVIN:
I'm staying here in this spot
Whether you want me to or not
I'm staying.

(*Fully dressed, he crawls into bed.*)

Here I am
By your side
One old horny lover.

WHIZZER:
Please go home and don't be scared.

MARVIN:
What's the fuss?
I'm not scared.
What good is a lover
Who's scared?
Hit me if you need to.
Slap my face, or
Hold me till winter.
Oh, baby, please do.
I love you too,
My lover.

WHIZZER:
Marvin, just go home and
Turn on TV.
Drink a little something till you're dead.
Think of me around
Sleeping soundly in our bed.
Marvin,
Did you hear what I said?

MARVIN:
Shut your mouth.
Go to sleep.
Time I met a sailor.
Are you sleeping yet, or
What is what?
Whizzer, but
I can't help but feeling
I've failed.
Let's be scared together.
Let's pretend that nothing is awful.

WHIZZER:
There's nothing to fear.

MARVIN:
There's nothing to fear.

WHIZZER:
Just stay right here.

BOTH:
I love you.

(DR. CHARLOTTE *and* CORDELIA *poke their heads in the door. They sing to each other a little too loud.*)

DR. CHARLOTTE:
Shhh. Maybe he's tired.

CORDELIA:
Shhh. Maybe he's waiting for us.

DR. CHARLOTTE:
Shhh. Maybe he's waiting for a visit?

(*They enter gingerly.*)

BOTH:
Is it a bad time?

(WHIZZER *starts laughing.*)

We'll come back. If it's a bad time,
We'll come back.

(MARVIN *waves them in.*)

We'll come in.

(*They join the men around the bed.*)

MARVIN:
Look at us.
Four old friends.
Four unlikely lovers.

CORDELIA:
We don't know what time will bring.

WHIZZER:
I've a clue.

MARVIN:
I have too.

WOMEN:
Let's look like we haven't.

ALL FOUR:
And each say nothing.

WHIZZER:
Sky.

DR. CHARLOTTE:
It's blue.

MARVIN:
I love the sky.

CORDELIA:
I love the trees.

MARVIN:
I love bad weather.

DR. CHARLOTTE:
I love the earth beneath my feet.

WHIZZER:
I love friends
That hover.

ALL FOUR:
Gee, we love to eat.
And we need something sweet
To love.
What a group
We four are.
Four unlikely lovers.
And we vow that we will
Buy the farm
Arm in arm.
Four unlikely lovers
With heart.
Let's be scared together.
Let's pretend that nothing
Is awful.   MARVIN:
There's nothing
To fear.   There's nothing to fear.
Just stay right here.
I love you.

                                 I love you.
I love you.
                                 I love you.

ALL FOUR:
Who'd have thought
That we four
Would end up as lovers?

Another Miracle of Judaism

JASON:
Hello, God.
I don't think we've ever really spoken.
If you'd kindly allow,
How about a miracle now?
I don't know if you exist.
I can't hear your fingers snappin'.
Are you just a big psychiatrist?
Or can you make things not happen?
Do this for me
And I'll get bar mitzvahed.
In exchange for:
Could you please make my friend stop dying?
I am not naive.
It won't be easy,
But if you could make my friend stop dying,
God,
That'd be the miracle of Judaism.
That'd be the miracle of Judaism.

Something Bad Is Happening (Reprise)

DR. CHARLOTTE (*outside the hospital room, to* MARVIN):
Something bad is happening.
Something very bad is happening.
Something that kills.
Something contagious.
Something that spreads
From one man to another.

You Gotta Die Sometime

WHIZZER:
Okay—
When the doctor started using phrases like
"You'll pass away,"
What could I say?
I said, Doctor,
In plain English,
Tell me why was I chosen,
Why me of all men?
Doctor,
Here's the good part:
At least death means
I'll never be scared about dying again.

Let's get on with living while we can
And not play dumb.
Death's gonna come.
When it does, screw the nerves,
I'll be eating hors d'oeuvres,
It's the roll of the dice and no crime,
You gotta die sometime.

Death is not a friend
But I hope in the end,
He takes me in his arms and lets me hold his face.
He holds me in his arms and whispers something
    funny.
He lifts me in his arms and tells me to embrace
His attack.
Then the scene turns to black.

Life sucks.
People always hate a loser
And they hate lame ducks.

Screw me and shucks.
That's it.
That's the ballgame.
I don't smoke, don't do drugs,
And then comes the bad news.
I quit.
That's the ballgame
It's the chink in the armor,
The shit in the karma,
The blues.
Can I keep my cool despite the urge
To fall apart?
How should I start?
I would cry if I could.
But it does no damn good
To explain I'm a man in my prime.
You gotta die sometime.

Death's a funny pal
With a weird sort of talent.
He puts his arms around my neck and walks me to the
  bed.
He pins me up against the wall and kisses me like
  crazy.
The many stupid things I thought about with dread
Now delight.
Then the scene turns to white.

Give me the balls to orchestrate
A graceful leave.
That's my reprieve:
To go out
Without care,
My head high
In the air,
It's the last little mountain I'll climb,

I'll climb.
You gotta die sometime.
You gotta die sometime.
You gotta die sometime.
You gotta die
Sometime, sometime,
Sometime, sometime,
Sometime, sometime,
Sometime, sometime.

(*Someone is knocking on the door.*)

Jason's Bar Mitzvah

(JASON *appears in the doorway.*)

JASON:
Whizzer, hey,
Suddenly it all came clear
I said, let's have my bar mitzvah here!

(*The champagne bottle he was holding behind his back is held out triumphantly.*)

ALL EXCEPT WHIZZER:
Surprise!

(*Behind* JASON, *the others stream in, loaded with flowers, food, candles, clothes, and decorations.*)

MARVIN:
This was Jason's first-rate idea.
And I brought the prayer shawl.

(Lovingly he throws the tallis around WHIZZER*'s shoulders.)*

ALL:
It's Jason's bar mitzvah.

MENDEL *(to* WHIZZER*)*:
Don't you move.
Everything will soon be great.
Close your eyes.
While we redecorate.

*(*TRINA *finds the camera.)*

CORDELIA:
I'll unwrap the billion hors d'oeuvres.
And someone please eat them.

TRINA *(gathering everyone and speaking)*:
Photo!

(Group ad lib.)

ALL:
It's Jason's bar mitzvah.

(More group photo ad lib.)

TRINA *(setting out the candles)*:
Lovely.
Flowers make things lovely.
Champagne makes things lovely too.
Something is amiss.

MENDEL *(passing around champagne)*:
Drink up.

Anyone for bubbly?

TRINA:
Probably it's doubly
Useful at a time like this.
Cheers.

MENDEL (*to* WHIZZER):
Cheers.

TRINA:
And aren't things lovely?
I feel more helpless than I have in years.

(MARVIN *hands* WHIZZER *a robe or a bag.*)

MARVIN:
Try this on.

(*Quietly to* MENDEL:)

Mendel, get this thing in gear.

WHIZZER:
Please excuse me
If I interfere,
But I feel that since I'm the host,
It's me who should toast him.

ALL EXCEPT JASON:
Oooh, oooh.

WHIZZER (*as everyone raises their glasses*):
To Jason's bar mitzvah.

(*Everyone leaves but the three women.*)

DR. CHARLOTTE:
I notified the nurses,
Told them please to not intrude.

CORDELIA:
I passed around the food
And dumped some extra food
'Cause, Lord knows, we've got plenty.

DR. CHARLOTTE:
She's cooked for some two hundred guests.

CORDELIA:
We number not that many.
Actually we're . . .

(*She stops to count. Pause.*)

Seven.

DR. CHARLOTTE:
Maybe it's not dumb
The way this whole thing ends.
The food tastes really yummy.

CORDELIA (*hugging* DR. CHARLOTTE):
Oh, Mummy.

(TRINA *can't believe what she's heard.*)

DR. CHARLOTTE AND
CORDELIA: TRINA:
The flowers seem to sparkle   Lovely.
Candelabra sets the tone.   I must make things
The wine is very soothing.

Soothes the "something
   something"
Someone needed soothing.

Lovely.
Put everything

DR. CHARLOTTE:
I think perhaps I'm overdressed.

In its place.

CORDELIA:
I think perhaps it doesn't matter
that you are, but

Ready for the

BOTH:
Here we are,
Jason's bar mitzvah looks
Like the books
Say it should.
Cheers.

band.

Cheers.
And aren't things

Everything is lovely.

Lovely?

(WHIZZER, *in his bar mitzvah robe, offers his arm to
escort* TRINA.)

DR. CHARLOTTE AND
CORDELIA:
I feel more rotten than I
   have in years.

TRINA:
I feel more rotten than I
   have in years.

MENDEL AND WHIZZER:
Here he comes.

MENDEL (*to* TRINA):
Fix his tie.

(JASON *enters, dressed in a black suit and solemn tie.*)

Trina, try
To make him smile more.

ALL EXCEPT MARVIN AND JASON:
Don't know why
But he looks like Marvin.

MARVIN (*to* JASON):
How did you turn out so great?
Who do I thank for the man you turned into?
Kid, do you know
How proud I am?
If I don't show
How proud I am . . .
You hold my dreams,
Kid, I burst at the seams
'Cause of you.

MENDEL:
Son of Abraham, Isaac, and Jacob.
Son of Marvin, son of Trina, son of Whizzer, son of
    Mendel,

ALL EXCEPT MENDEL:
And godchild to the lesbians from next door,

MENDEL:
Sing.
Oh-oh, sing.
Oh-oh, sing.

JASON:
Vie-eme-low yae-o-leh.
Heh-oh-non vi-low.
Ah-yis-is-ooh ay-ysi-ro-ale.
Ha-ooh low toe vo-o-meem aboh.

(WHIZZER *can't go on anymore, and taps* JASON *as he leaves, escorted by* DR. CHARLOTTE. *Everyone else but Marvin follows.*)

What Would I Do?

MARVIN (*left alone*):
What would I do
If I had not met you?
Who would I blame my life on?
Once I was told
That all men get what they deserve.
Who the hell then threw this curve?
There are no answers.
But who would I be
If you had not been my friend?

You're the only one,
One out of a thousand others,
Only one my child would allow.
When I'm having fun,
You're the one I wanna talk to.
Where have you been?
Where are you now?

(WHIZZER *appears behind* MARVIN, *dressed as we first saw him.* MARVIN *turns around, sees* WHIZZER *and catches his breath.*)

What would I do
If I had not loved you?
How would I know what love is?
God only knows, too soon
I'll remember your faults.
Meanwhile, though, it's tears and schmaltz.

There are no answers.
But what would I do
If you had not been my friend?

WHIZZER:
All your life you wanted men,
And when you got it up to have them,
Who knew it could end your life?

MARVIN:
I left my kid and left my wife
To be with you,
To be insulted by such handsome men.

(*They face each other.*)

WHIZZER:
Do you regret—?

MARVIN (*stopping him*):
I'd do it again.
I'd like to believe that I'd do it again
And again and again . . .
And
What more can I say?

WHIZZER:
What more can I say?

MARVIN:
How am I to face tomorrow?

BOTH:
After being screwed out of today.
Tell me what's in store.

MARVIN:
Yes, I'd beg or steal or borrow
If I could hold you for
One hour more.

WHIZZER: MARVIN:
One hour more.

                                      One hour more.

One hour more.
One hour, one hour more.   One hour, one hour more.

MARVIN:
What would I do

WHIZZER:
What would I do

MARVIN:
If I had not seen you?

WHIZZER:
If I had not seen you?

BOTH:
Who would I feast my eyes on?
Once I was told
That good men get better with age.

MARVIN:
We're just gonna skip that stage.

There are no answers.
But what would I do
If you hadn't been my friend?

WHIZZER:
There are no answers.
But what would I do . . .

(WHIZZER *exits*.)

MARVIN:
No simple answers.
But what would I do
If you had not been
My friend.
My friend.
My friend.

(*First* JASON, *then everyone else gathers around*
MARVIN.)

MENDEL:
Homosexuals.
Women with children.
Short insomniacs.
We're a teeny tiny band.
Lovers come and lovers go.
Lovers live and die fortissimo.
This is where we take a stand.
Welcome to Falsettoland.

(DR. CHARLOTTE *walks in and joins the circle at the
same time as* MENDEL. TRINA *consoles* MARVIN.)

(*Fade to black.*)

"IN TROUSERS"

For Barbara Finn, Jason Finn,
Nancy Finn Davis, and Michael Finn

"IN TROUSERS" opened off-Broadway at the Promenade Theatre, run by Ben Sprecher, on March 26, 1985. It was produced by Roger Berlind, Franklin R. Levy, and Gregory Harrison and directed by Matt Casella. The setting was designed by Santo Loquasto, lighting by Marilyn Rennagel, costumes by Madeline Ann Graneto, and sound by Tom Morse. The musical direction was by Roy Leake, Jr., and the orchestrations by Michael Starobin. The cast was as follows:

Marvin...Stephen Bogardus
Trina, his wife ....Catherine Cox
His high school sweetheart ....Sherry Hursey
His teacher, Miss Goldberg
(who always wears sunglasses) ....Kathy Garrick

An earlier version of the musical was produced by Playwrights Horizons in 1979 with the following cast:

Marvin.. Chip Zien
Trina, his wife ....Alison Fraser
His high school sweetheart ....Joanna Green
His teacher, Miss Goldberg
(who always wears sunglasses) ....Mary Testa

This version was directed by William Finn. The orchestration and musical direction were by Michael Starobin.

The version you are reading is a combination of the two.

Very Opening

LADIES:
We don't even know why people laugh anymore.
In Trousers.

MARVIN (*speaking*):
I mean, everybody always talks about love, but nobody
ever does anything about it.

LADIES:
In Trousers.

MARVIN (*speaking*):
Except for Marvin. You see, this is an upbeat show.

LADIES:
In Trousers.

MARVIN:
One, two. One, two, three. One, two, three, four.

Marvin's Giddy Seizures

MARVIN:
Marvin is a boy who has giddy seizures,
I'm laughing all the time.
Marvin is a boy who has giddy seizures,
Sometimes they're fatal.

When I turn upside down like a ladle pouring soup
I'm a veritable fool.
Marvin is my very best friend in school.
It's me and Marvin.

Lately I've been thinking maybe Marvin needs
    attention
Of a private sort.
Maybe this whole seizure thing is something I
    invented,
Or is it medicinal: should my mother be blamed?

ALL:
Marvin has a something which most everybody needs;
He cannot ever be embarrassed.

MARVIN:
Marvin is my very best friend in school.
And I'm embarrassed and ashamed. Oh.

LADIES (*all at once*):
Marvin! What are you doing?
Who do you think you are, Marvin?
What's Marvin doing?

MARVIN:
Pardon me, boys and girls, but I'm having a seizure.

LADIES:
Oh, Marvin. Hey, Marvin.

MARVIN:
Yes, I'm having a seizure today, hey, hey,
Watch me laugh.

LADIES:
Marvin's giddy seizures.

MARVIN:
Watch me cry.

LADIES:
Marvin's giddy seizures.

MARVIN:
I am counting on your prayers to get me by.

LADIES:
Marvin's giddy seizures.

MARVIN:
Well, my arms disappear and my legs disappear and
    my knees disappear and my shoulders disappear
When Marvin throws the best fit of the year.

ALL:
Marvin's giddy seizures: Marvin needs love.
He needs love. He needs love.
He needs love. Ooooooh.

MARVIN:
Marvin holds his breath, his face is under water
But that's not a seizure.
Marvin talks of death, he simulates a slaughter
But that's not a seizure.
Then he begins to shriek like a virgin,
And his eyes turn an ordinary fizz—
(Nothing is exactly like I say it is)—
But hey, that's a seizure.

(MARVIN *is getting into bed.*)

LADIES (*all at once*):
Marvin, what are you doing?
Who do you think you are, Marvin?
What's Marvin doing?

MARVIN:
Pardon me, boys and girls, but I'm having a seizure.

LADIES:
Oh, Marvin. Hey, Marvin.

MARVIN:
Yes, I'm having a seizure today, hey, hey, hey, hey,
   hey.
Watch me laugh.

LADIES:
Marvin's giddy seizures.

MARVIN:
Watch me cry.

LADIES:
Marvin's giddy seizures.

MARVIN:
I am counting on your prayers to get me by.

LADIES:
Marvin's giddy seizures.
Arms.

MARVIN:
Disappear.

LADIES:
Legs.

MARVIN:
Disappear.

LADIES:
Groin.

MARVIN:
Disappears.

LADIES:
Knees.

MARVIN:
Disappear
When Marvin throws the best fit of the year.

ALL:
Marvin's giddy seizures: Marvin needs love.
He needs love. He needs love.
He needs love. Ooooooh.

Marvin's giddy seizures. Marvin needs love.
He needs love. He needs love.
He needs love. Ooooooh.

Marvin's giddy seizures. Marvin needs love.
He needs love. He needs love.
He needs love. Ooooooh.

A Helluva Day

(MARVIN *is sleeping and* TRINA *is trying to wake him.*)

TRINA (*carrying a glass of wine and an alarm clock*):
It's a helluva day.
It's a wonderful morning.
What a wonderful way
To say all's fine.
It's your moment to shine.
Just forget last night.
This itty-bitty glass of wine
Helps us start our day out right.
Now come and eat your *petit déjeuner.*
Time to wake up.
Time to wake up, Marvin,
And face the day.
Listen my grace,
Our ten-year-old is crying.
Please show your face.

It's a nice easy hour.
Soon I'm belting our child.
In an hour it's time to climb the walls.
If our ten-year-old crawls,
How should I react?
I think he plays with girls and dolls.
Who can know what love he's lacked?
But me, I try to send
Those blues away.
Time to wake up.
Time to wake up, Marvin,
And face the day.
Time to wake up.
Time to—

MARVIN:
What time is it?

(*A venetian blind is raised to reveal* MISS GOLDBERG
and MARVIN'S HIGH SCHOOL SWEETHEART.)

MISS GOLDBERG:
Time . . .
To wake up.
Time to wake
    up, Marvin,
Time to wake
    up, Marvin,
Time to wake up.

	TRINA:	SWEETHEART:
Time . . .	Time to wake up.	Time to wake up, Marvin,

To wake up.
Time to wake   And face the day.
    up,
Marvin,
Time to wake
    up, Marvin,
Time to wake up.

(*Quietly:*)	(*Quietly:*)	(*Not quietly:*)
Time . . .	Time to wake up.	We . . .
	Time to wake up, Marvin,	Can't stand here, Marvin,
To wake up,		
	And face the day.	Waiting forever.
Time to wake up, Marvin,		
Time to wake up.		So, move your ass, Marvin!

LADIES:
Time to wake up.
Time to wake up, Marvin . . .
And face the day.

(*They disappear.*)

I Have a Family

(MARVIN *sits up in bed and explains.*)

MARVIN:
Something's missing
In my life.
I don't know what it is.
Though I've suspicions
I cannot act on them because . . .

I have a family.
And a family pet.
And a family that will get upset
When it learns why I show stress.

I have a family
With a wife who's perfect in many ways,
And a dazzling son
Who will set the world ablaze.

Still I can smell
There's trouble brewing.
How can I tell
That something's doing?
Something's missing.
In my mind I'm kissing
Men . . .
No. No. No. No. Start again.

(*A big smile.*)

I have a family.
Which I've never defiled.
But I'm honest when I say I'm a child
For a fella's caress.
Pardon me while I regress.

How Marvin Eats His Breakfast

(MARVIN *regresses to himself at an earlier age.*)

MARVIN:
I love being Marvin. I love being Marvin. Marvin always eats the finest breakfast in town.

LADIES (*dressed as maids*):
How Marvin eats his breakfast.

MARVIN:
Everybody into the kitchen.
Here comes Marvin.
Banging his groin with his fist.

LADIES:
He mumbles in, to insist:

MARVIN:
No one looks busy in this kitchen
And my breakfast isn't ready
And my stomach aches.
I mean specifically the maid
Who is reclining like she's laid the golden egg.
I want some chatter and some gruel,
Make me wanna drool,

Try to make me hungry.
Cat got your tongue?

LADIES:
Marvin always knows the sort of answers he'll allow.

MARVIN:
I may be sly, dear, but not young.

LADIES:
"Wait until I'm older—then I'll kill you" is his one un-
    spoken vow.

MARVIN:
I need my breakfast now.

ALL:
Everybody into the kitchen,
Here comes Marvin.

LADIES:
Aiming a gun at the maid;
He shoots her head; she falls dead.

MARVIN:
Oh, Jesus Christ, it wasn't loaded.
She's an actor from the old school
And a lousy chef.
I don't want miracles from heaven—
Just some eggies over spinach
Over toast.

No, I will not apologize!
She should win a prize:
Very Best Emoting.

That girl can't cook.

LADIES:
Maybe she can't cook, but have you seen her milk a
  cow?

MARVIN:
And I can read her like a book.

LADIES:
Marvin wouldn't read that kind of novel anyhow.

MARVIN:
I need my breakfast
Now.

People, people (people, people)
Stop your staring (stop your staring)
People, people, stop your staring
Get to work, my breakfast isn't made yet.

ALL:
Life is lonely
Life is rotten

MARVIN:
And thankfully short, thankfully short,
Thankfully short

LADIES:
Like Marvin.

MARVIN:
Everybody into the kitchen,
Here comes M-M-M-M-M—

LADIES:
Marvin.
Waving his hands like a twit.
He throws a fit,
Then a knife.

MARVIN:
You call this breakfast on my birthday?
This is shit
(This isn't breakfast)
I could crack your feet.

I mean for God's sake
Am I talking to the wall when I say breakfast
I mean food.

I dreamt all night of hips and legs,
Now I want some eggs—
Things I might relate to.

I'm just a sprite

LADIES:
Marvin underestimates the fear that he'll endow.

MARVIN:
I'll wait here till you get it right!

LADIES:
Do I? Do I really? Do I really have to show you people
   how?

MARVIN:
I need my breakfast

ALL:
NOOOOOOOW!

My High School Sweetheart

SWEETHEART:
My high school sweetheart is a person too.
I tell him he's a person.
He says I'm just ridickalous.
My high school sweetheart is a too ridickalous
    sweetheart
Who's a (who's a) person too.
He's a person.

I say a person has his wants and needs.
I'm not a greedy person.
He says I'm just ridickalous.
My high school sweetheart is a too ridickalous
    sweetheart
Who's a (who's a) person too.
He's a person.

TRINA AND MISS GOLDBERG:
He's a person.

SWEETHEART:
I'm a person.

TRINA AND MISS GOLDBERG:
He's a person.

SWEETHEART:
I'm a person.

MARVIN.
I'm a person.

SWEETHEART, TRINA, MISS GOLDBERG:
He's a person.

MARVIN:
I'm a person.

TRINA AND MISS GOLDBERG:
He's a person.

SWEETHEART:
I'm a person.

MARVIN:
She's a person.

SWEETHEART:
I'm a person.

TRINA AND MISS GOLDBERG:
He's a person.

MARVIN:
I'm a person.

SWEETHEART:
I'm a person.

TRINA:
I'm a person.

MARVIN:
I'm a person.

LADIES:
Marvin loves Miss Goldberg.

SWEETHEART:
And I'm his sweetheart.

MARVIN: TRINA:
I love Miss Goldberg.
She cast me in her play.
She gave me words to say.
Made me what I am today.
I am Columbus.   I'm a person.
Columbus.   I'm a person.
King of the Ocean.   I'm a person.

ALL:
Columbus.

MARVIN (*speaking*):
Christopher Columbus, you may recall, had three ships:
   the Nina, the Pinta, and the Santa Maria, the Santa
   Maria being the best-looking of the three, lots of
   gold and carved wood. Even the Pinta had its admir-
   ers. But it was the Nina that Christopher was fondest
   of, 'cause it reminded him of his mother—Nina
   Columbus.

MISS GOLDBERG:
Go ahead. Play Columbus. Stop begging.
Stop making me crazy, Marvin. Crazy Marvin.
I love the way Marvin acts. I do.
Do not make faces and do not undo the facts.
Relax. Relax. Relax. Relax.

(*Speaking*):

Queen Isabella—this is not often told to sixth grad-
   ers—but here goes:

MARVIN (*speaking*):
Queen Isabella, who financed Columbus' trip to
  America, was his secret girlfriend.

TRINA AND SWEETHEART (*speaking*):
A historical fact.

MARVIN (*speaking*):
He was her date at a cotillion given by Spanish society on the occasion of her inauguration. But because he wasn't royalty, he was made to sit upstairs
  in her bedroom. And while she cavorted downstairs,
  he read back issues of *Stella d'oro* and other
  fifteenth-century periodicals.

MISS GOLDBERG (*angry*):
What?

MARVIN (*speaking*):
Columbus later said, "It was one of the best nights of
  my life."

LADIES (*singing*):
He loves Miss Goldberg.

MARVIN:
She cast me in her play.
She gave me words to say.
Made me what I am today.

TRINA:
I'm a person.
I'm a person.

MARVIN:
I am Columbus.

Columbus.
King of the Ocean.

MISS GOLDBERG:
Go ahead. Play Columbus. Stop begging.
Stop making me crazy, Marvin. Crazy Marvin.
I love the way Marvin acts. I do.
Do not make faces and do not undo the facts.

SWEETHEART:
I'm his sweetheart. I'm his sweetheart.

ALL:
Columbus.

MARVIN (*speaking*):
Columbus's last words were: "I only wish I could have
   discovered Europe." Which brings my study of Columbus to a fitting end.

Set Those Sails

MISS GOLDBERG:
The world is round.
There's a key to every door.
That's what our hero found.
Nothing is for nothing, and a new land is a new land to
   explore,
Not just paths you retrace.
I'm talking mountains and space.

Hey, I love you. Set those sails.
A good man never fails.

Watch me close, close your eyes.
I am living proof that cowards still can rise.
You might tell me you're a victim.

You might get what you deserve.
But I won't excuse.
Boy, I can't excuse,
A boy who's lost his nerve.

O Lord, set sail.
Be preparing for a fall.
Stay clear of love and jail;
Lovers don't go hungry, and the appetite of young men
 counts for all.
Lord, it's rough in the sack.
Kid, live and learn to attack.

Hey, I love you.
Set those sails.
A good man never fails.

Hey, I love you.
Set those sails.
A good man never fails.

TRINA AND SWEETHEART:
Hey, I love you.
Set those sails.
A good man never fails.

Hey, I love you.
Set those sails.
A good man never fails.

(*The singing has become a
big gospel wail.*)

Hey, I love you.
Set those sails.
A good man never fails.

My Chance to Survive the Night

LADIES:
Relax. Relax. Relax. Relax.
Relax. Relax. Relax.

TRINA:
Relax, Marvin.

MARVIN:
Here's my chance to survive the night.
There's nothing special about it;
If I try to go to sleep I might, but the phone will ring.
I had a girl.
She cut her lip on the sofa by the door.
The sofa was blue before.
That's it for girls. That's it for girls.
Here's my chance to survive, to survive the night.

Here's a dance
I might try to make.
I'm not so lucid about it
But I'm sure of the path that the arms must take
And the feet don't move.
I found a word.
It was a queer little thing with lots of regret.
I had a way with words and yet
I'm through with words.
That's it for words.
Here's my chance to survive, to survive the night,
Here's my chance to survive, to survive the night,
To survive the day, to survive my life
In the most very natural, most unremarkable way.

I played a game.
She was as cute as a dime and couldn't spell.
I asked her to spell my name.
That's it for girls. That's it for girls. That's it for girls.
That's it, that's it, that's it for girls,
That's it, that's it, that's it for girls.
Here is my chance to survive, to survive the night.
Here's my chance to survive, to survive the night.

Here's my chance to survive, survive, survive, survive,
   to survive the night.

High-Heeled Ladies at Five O'Clock
(A Calypso Fantasy)

HIGH-HEELED SWEETHEART (*often joined by other*
LADIES):
High-heeled ladies at five o'clock:
We be good girls all,
Practicing adventures of a sort
Which divert you
But which never ever try to hurt you.
High-heeled ladies at five o'clock.
We sing la la la la la la la
We sing la la la la
(Oh how they repetitious)
La la la la mumble and walk
You see them: high-heeled ladies at five o'clock.

Sacrifice the pain, sacrifice the worry.
We be waiting in the street
Underneath the local fire engine.
Tap us on the feet and we go for a walk
Just mention high-heeled ladies at five o'clock.
We sing la la la la la la la
We sing la la la la
(Oh how they repetitious)
La la la la mumble and squawk (but meet us)
High-heeled ladies at five o'clock.

(*Variation, then together, then:*)

High-heeled (high-heeled) ladies at five o'clock

(High-heeled) high-heeled (ladies at five o'clock)
High-heeled (high-heeled) ladies at five o'clock
Hoichy chumbo, hoichy chumbo, hoichy chumbo
High-heeled (high-heeled) ladies at five o'clock
(High-heeled) high-heeled (ladies at five o'clock)
High-heeled (high-heeled) ladies at five o'clock.

SWEETHEART:
Does he like the rain?

TRINA AND MISS GOLDBERG:
Oh yes he do.

SWEETHEART:
Is he better than banana?

MARVIN:
Aaaaaah.

SWEETHEART:
Does he like the snow?

TRINA AND MISS GOLDBERG:
Oh yes he do.

SWEETHEART:
Is he better than banana?

MARVIN:
Aaaaaah.

SWEETHEART:
Does he laugh?

MARVIN:
No.

SWEETHEART:
Touch?

MARVIN:
No.

SWEETHEART:
Drink.

MARVIN:
No.

SWEETHEART:
Screw?

MARVIN:
No.

SWEETHEART:
High-heeled ladies at nine a.m.
We be waiting at the school,
We admirin' the photograph
Of Marvin on the stage,
Turn the page and look at
High-heeled ladies at five o'clock.
(Does he like?) Does he like?
(Does he like to screw?)
Does he like? (Does he like?)
Does he like to screw?
(Does he like?) Does he like?
(Does he like to screw his friends?)
Does he?

TRINA AND MISS GOLDBERG:
Does he?

MARVIN:
Does he?

LADIES:
(Does he like?) Does he like?
(Does he like to screw?)
Does he like? (Does he like?)
Does he like to screw?
(Does he like?) Does he like?
(Does he like to screw?)

MARVIN:
DOES HE?!

(MARVIN *is threatening the* SWEETHEART.)

The Rape of Miss Goldberg by Marvin
(A Fantasy Which Is Better Abstracted)

SWEETHEART (*speaking*):
"The Rape of Miss Goldberg"—by Marvin.
Scene one.

MARVIN:
Hi, Miss Goldberg at your desk.
My name's Marvin, we're alone at last.
I turned fourteen just today
And I thought for a not unseemly price,
You'd introduce me to the wonders of the bed
And also treat me nice.

I'm the boy who throws the fits.
He who puts the chalk inside his ear.
Do you know me from a hole in the wall?

Marvin's cute though rarely good.
But, dearest, please accept my hand
Miss Goldberg who
Is perfect womanhood.

SWEETHEART (*speaking*):
Scene two.

MISS GOLDBERG:
Marvin, how,
Tell me how did you get in here, please?

MARVIN:
I drugged the man who was guarding the floor.

MISS GOLDBERG:
Marvin, open up the door.
Marvin, please turn on the light.
Marvin, listen,
I'm the only one here in the school
Except you,
And the guard who you beat in a fight.

MARVIN:
He was drugged.

MISS GOLDBERG:
He was drugged.

MARVIN:
Not with pills.

MISS GOLDBERG:
Then with what?

MARVIN:
With some apples from a basket.
Would you like a few, Miss Goldberg?
What I do for you, Miss Goldberg,
Is your pleasure.

SWEETHEART (*speaking*):
Scene three.

MISS GOLDBERG:
Why should Marvin jump on Miss Goldberg?
Why does Marvin dump on Miss Goldberg?
I knew,
When I first looked in his eyes.

MARVIN:
I like your eyes, Miss Goldberg.

MISS GOLDBERG:
Lies!
He has never seen my face.

MARVIN:
I have never seen your eyes.

MISS GOLDBERG:
I was never out of place.
I taught.

MARVIN:
That's true.
She minded her business.
She taught . . .

MISS GOLDBERG:
. . . I taught and I minded my business.

MARVIN:
But the business at hand . . .

MISS GOLDBERG:
Keep your hands off my eyes!

MARVIN:
But the business at hand . . .

MISS GOLDBERG:
Keep your hands off my eyes!

MARVIN:
But the business at hand
Is . . .

SWEETHEART (*speaking*):
Scene four.

MARVIN:
I always liked the way you wore your glasses.
In and out of classes.
I always liked the way you got angry in your glasses.
That's cool,
Miss Goldberg.
I always thought those glasses hid your passion.
That's Miss Goldberg's fashion, I said.
Now it's my birthday and here's my surprise:
I'm gonna see your eyes, Miss Goldberg.
I'm gonna see your eyes, my darling!

MISS GOLDBERG:
Don't touch my goddamn eyes,
You little shit,
I'll throw a fit.
I'll beat your head in with a hammer!

SWEETHEART (*laughs; speaking*):
Scene five.

MISS GOLDBERG:
My eyes are my eyes.
Your hands are your hands.
Just keep your dirty fingers away from my face, kid.
That's the only thing Miss Goldberg demands.

MARVIN (*speaking*):
Now move.

SWEETHEART (*speaking*):
Scene six.

MARVIN (*speaking*):
Now move! *Now move!*

(*Singing:*)

Listen, I'm a bastard.
Bummer with a penis
And I mean us two to be together,
Teacher, yes I do, I do.
I mean us two to screw together,
Me together
You together.
Miss Goldberg?

MISS GOLDBERG:
What?

MARVIN:
Miss Goldberg?

MISS GOLDBERG:
What?

MARVIN:
Make Marvin a happy boy!

(MISS GOLDBERG *screams*.)

SWEETHEART (*speaking*):
Scene seven! One, two, three, four!

MARVIN: MISS GOLDBERG:
Miss Goldberg,
Miss Goldberg,
Miss Goldberg,
Miss Goldberg,
Please, please, please,
Rub your hands between
Your hands between my
  knees . . .
La, la, la, la   What does Marvin
La, la, la, la   Want from Miss Goldberg?
La, la, la, la   What does Marvin
La, la, la, la   Want from Miss Goldberg?
Miss Goldberg, Miss   What does Marvin
  Goldberg
Miss Goldberg, Miss   Want from Miss Goldberg?
  Goldberg
Please, please, please,   What does Marvin
  please
Please, please, please,   Want from Miss Goldberg?
  please
Please, please, please,   What does Marvin
  please
Please, please, please,   Want from Miss Goldberg?
  please
Please!!

SWEETHEART (*speaking*):
Scene eight.

MARVIN:
Marvin always gets the things
He wants.

MISS GOLDBERG:
Except the things
He wants.

MARVIN:
He gets the things
He wants.

MISS GOLDBERG: MARVIN:
Marvin
Always gets the things   Marvin
He wants   Always
Except the   Gets the
Things he wants.   Things he wants.

MARVIN:
He gets the things . . .

MISS GOLDBERG:
Except the things . . .

MARVIN:
He gets the things . . .

MISS GOLDBERG:
Except the things . . .

MARVIN AND MISS GOLDBERG:
He . . .

SWEETHEART:
Wants . . .

MARVIN (*having removed the sunglasses from* MISS
GOLDBERG'*s eyes*):
Do you want my telephone number?

(MISS GOLDBERG *looks absolutely desolate like, in fact, she'd been raped.*)

SWEETHEART (*speaking*):
Curtain!

I Am Wearing a Hat

(*At the wedding of* MARVIN *to* TRINA.)

MISS GOLDBERG (*to* SWEETHEART):
Watch Marvin as he takes his bride.
This whole damn thing's a joke.
Before the act is sanctified
Perhaps he'll trip or she might choke.
Forget this guy, he's no damn good . . .
No action and all words . . .
Marvin is sometimes for the birds.

SWEETHEART (*seriously drunk*):
Hide my face.
Change my place of worship.
Call me a disgrace
And then be done with blame.
How was I to know
That he's a gigolo
Emotionally underbred?
When the passion stings
I think of pretty things
Instead.

I am wearing a hat.
After winter, I'll marry.
I'm entitled to that.
I wear a hat.
I wear a hat.

Here I sit.
Drunk and self-indulgent.
Dressed up in a hat which even I detest.

SWEETHEART AND MISS GOLDBERG:
Marry money,
Money wins.
Your past will disappear
And with it all your sins.
Joy once seemed so near,
Now what's left to fear
Begins.

MISS GOLDBERG:
I am wearing
A hat.
He'd approve
If I let him.
Since the world's
Come to that.
I wear a hat.

SWEETHEART:

I am wearing
A hat.
After winter
I'll marry.
I'm entitled
To wear a hat.

(TRINA *marches on in her wedding gown.*)

MISS GOLDBERG AND SWEETHEART:
I remember my place.
Though it's hard to forget him.
But he can't see my face.
I wear a hat.
I wear a hat.

TRINA:
I wear a . . . hat.

(*She looks for* MARVIN *offstage and says:*)

Marvin?

LADIES:
Hat!

Wedding Song (Part 1)

SWEETHEART AND MISS GOLDBERG:
Where's her goddamn husband?
Where's the goddamn aisle?
Always acting infantile.
That's one thing that makes him smile.

(MARVIN *is pushed onstage.*)

MARVIN:
I do not think that this will work.
I think we should've spoke before.
But today's too late.
I hate weddings.

SWEETHEART AND MISS GOLDBERG:
We love weddings.

SWEETHEART:
Is her veil on straight?

MISS GOLDBERG:
And is she drunk?

SWEETHEART:
I hope so.

MISS GOLDBERG:
Does he look at her?

SWEETHEART (*hopefully*):
Or look away?

MISS GOLDBERG:
I do not know the answer.

TRINA:
Will you be the man I've dreamt about?

MISS GOLDBERG AND SWEETHEART:
Isn't this a perfect day?

Three Seconds

MARVIN (*deadpan*):
What should I think about
Five seconds before I die?
Will the maid unpaid
Still come Tuesday?
Did I pick my laundry up
Wednesday night?
And there's some milk
Rotting
In my refrigerator.
Rotting and stinking up the other food
Of which there isn't much
Because I'm about to die
And I didn't feel like shopping.

(*Rimshot*)

What do I think about
Four seconds before I die?
Did I say goodbye
To the girls from

High school?

SWEETHEART AND MISS
GOLDBERG:
Bye.

What do they want?

Bye. bye.

Is that enough for them?

Bye. bye. bye.

Bye.

Bye . . .

Bye.

Bye, bye.

(*To* SWEETHEART AND MISS GOLDBERG):

Please stop your bye-ing.
Have pity on one who's dying.
Four seconds my heart will stop.
Four seconds I close up shop. Hey!

What do I think about?
What do I think
What do I
What do I
What do I
What do I
What do I
What do I

What do I think about
Three seconds before I die?
When her passion soon cools—
And it will . . . if she's smart.
Will she countenance fools?
Will I end what I start?
Will I break a few rules?
Will I break the girl's heart?

Did I ever have . . . ?
No. Did I ever have . . .
Will I ever have fun?

LADIES:
Three.
Two.
One.

(*Machine-gun fire.* MARVIN *screams. Silence. He opens his eyes. Feels his pulse. He walks dejectedly back to the wedding.*)

Wedding Song (Part 2)

MISS GOLDBERG (*as the rabbi*):
Do you take
This woman
To be your wife?

MARVIN:
I do.
Yes, I do.
Yes, I . . .

MISS GOLDBERG:
Do you take this man to be your husband?

TRINA:
Yes, I doooo.
Yes, I doooooo.

MARVIN:
I do too.

(MARVIN *stamps down to break the glass. He misses. Tries again. Misses.* TRINA *breaks the glass.*)

MARVIN (*ruefully*):
Mazel tov.

How the Body Falls Apart

(MARVIN *is charmingly tearing* TRINA'S *wedding gown from her body: first the arms, then down from the neckline, until by the end of the song she looks totally undone.*)

LADIES:
How the body falls apart:
First the groin and then the heart.
It's easy
And it's smart.
Things on which we most depend
Seem to fail us in the end.
How like
Like a body
When the body
Falls
Apart.

I Feel Him Slipping Away

(*Time passes.*)

TRINA:
We've been married for ten years.
Eight were fine; and six were not.

It seemed longer than ten years.
What I recall is better forgot.

The first two were the best years:
When the kid was born,
When the world seemed okay.

But I
I felt him slipping away.
I felt him die in my arms,
His charms
Were not for me.
How could I ever compete?
The cause of all his lust—
She must
Be sweet . . .

And maybe too old.
She might have a limp.
Or she might have
Acne, or polio, or something.

If the lady's just an ass—
Say she dotes on cops and G-men—
Let's suppose she's lower-class—
How'd he choose her over me then?

He used to love me.
He used to love me.
He used to love me.

MISS GOLDBERG (*speaking*):
Ah, don't be pathetic.

SWEETHEART (*speaking*):
She's so pathetic.

TRINA:
Is it hard to deceive me?
No, just bring a note from home.
He could just as well leave me;
When he's with us,
He's somewhere alone.

MISS GOLDBERG AND SWEETHEART:
You'll be fine.

TRINA:
I'll be fine if he leaves me.
But I'm sure he won't.
Trouble is we don't say.
But I . . .

MISS GOLDBERG, SWEETHEART, TRINA:
I felt him slipping away.
I felt him die in my arms,
His charms
Were not for me.
No. No. No. No. No.
How
Could I ever compete?
The cause of all his lust—
She must
Be sweet.

TRINA:
The bitch might be dumb.
She might think he's Kris Kringle.
And honest.
And single.

SWEETHEART AND MISS GOLDBERG:
He will not admit the truth.

TRINA:
He thinks I might like surprise.

SWEETHEART AND MISS GOLDBERG:
Why are men so damn uncouth?

TRINA:
Oh . . .

ALL:
All they ever tell are lies!

TRINA:
I feel him slipping away
I feel him dead in my arms.
His charms
Are not for me.
How
Can I ever compete?
The cause of all his lust—
She must
Be sweet . . .

LIAR!

Whizzer Going Down

(MARVIN *remembers the first time he had sex with a
man.*)

MARVIN:
He hates my wife.
I hate his food.
He thinks I'm rude but nice.
I think he's nice but indiscreet.

He thinks I'm sweet,
But he treats me kind of funny.
I say Whizzer, Whizzer Brown.
I see Whizzer, going down.

Oh, Whizzer, Whizzer Brown,
Isn't it delightful playing easy?
Yes, Whizzer, Whizzer Brown,
I care.
I found your door.
We sing out more
And more
And more
And more
And more now.

He rubs my neck.
I rub his thigh.
He asks me why I sweat.
I ask him why he bites his nails.
And then he takes me in his arms
And then he lights another cigarette.
I say Whizzer, Whizzer Brown.
I see Whizzer, going down.

Oh, Whizzer, Whizzer Brown,
Isn't it delightful playing easy?
Yes, Whizzer, Whizzer Brown,
I care.
We sing out more
And more
And more
And more
And more now.
Go, Whizzer.
How about, Whizzer?

Breathe deep, Whizzer.
Up and he's going down.

SWEETHEART AND MISS GOLDBERG:
Go, Whizzer.
How about, Whizzer?
Breathe deep, Whizzer.
Up and he's going down.

MARVIN:
He's on his knees.
I'm lying flat.
Just like a bad idea.
He starts to blow.
I start to fight.
The room is yellow and the bed is white.
He's going down.
I think I'll die away.
He's going down.
I think I'll die, die, die.
I say Whizzer . . .
Whizzer Brown.
I see Whizzer . . .

LADIES:
Whizzer . . .

MARVIN:
Going down.

(*Dance break—with scat vocals.*)

MARVIN:
He's going down.

SWEETHEART AND MISS GOLDBERG:
He's going down.

MARVIN:
He's going down.

SWEETHEART AND MISS GOLDBERG:
He's going down.

MARVIN:
He's going down.

SWEETHEART AND MISS GOLDBERG:
He's going down.

MARVIN:
Go, Whizzer.
Down!

ALL THREE:
Down!

A Breakfast Over Sugar

WIFE:
Pass the sugar, please.
I dreamt last night we
   flew to China.
Your parents own a car,
Don't they?
Won't they drive away?

MARVIN:

The sugar,
   please.

May we talk as friends?
I dreamt last night you al-
    most held me.
I cry as if on cue.
Hold me.
Hold him too.
But stay.

Please drink your tea be-
    fore it's cold.

I can't believe
We've
Worked

To end up this way.

Strip me down but stay.

Please.

Please.

Pass the sugar,
    please.

Please.

Please.
Jeez-us Christ, you'll come
    through.

Please drink your tea be-
    fore it's cold.

Pass the sugar, please.
You can't go on as if
    you're dying.

A martyr just won't play.

Hit me.
Strip me down but say:

This is much better for the
    both of us.
Now things are better for
    the both of us.

Please.
Please.

(*Drowning out the last lines of the song is the blasting
voice of a radio announcer.* MARVIN *forgets* TRINA *and
listens as she clears the tea things.*)

ANNOUNCER:
A hundred people in the stadium, cheering, booing in

the stands, the best of any year, the greatest of . . .
(*overlapping*) Five hundred people in the stands, laughing, the best of any year . . . (*overlapping*) Five thousand people in the stands, on their feet, watching the
best of any year . . . (*overlapping*) Five hundred thousand people in the stands, on their feet . . . (*overlapping*) Five million people in the stands, watching,
cheering . . . (*loud cheering, then subsiding into the
next song.*)

The Nausea Before the Game

MARVIN:
It's the nausea before the game
And the pain that won't subside in winter.
It's the knees that threaten to go bad
The body that you thought you had, that lied.
It's the scores that go unanswered and unsatisfied:
The growing up, the falling down, the throwing up, the
    shame,
The silent prayers, the nausea, the game.

It's anxiety when you recall
Girls who touch you when you're walking down the
    hall.
Nausea before the game, nausea before the game.

LADIES:
It's the promise of a perfect life, a perfect house, a per-
    fect wife she'll be.

MARVIN:
It's the promise of a perfect star
Who's me.

ALL:
The growing up, the falling down,
The throwing up, the shame,
The silent prayers, the nausea,
The game.

MARVIN:
The sneaking in, the passing out,
And where to place the blame,
The dying swans, the nausea,
The game.

ALL:
Nanananana nausea.
Nahoodyooayahsoblue.
Nanananananausea.
Nanananananausea.

(MARVIN *stands as quarterback*, TRINA *as center*.)

MARVIN:
Hut!

(TRINA *hikes the ball.* MARVIN *bobbles and drops it.*)

LADIES:
Pray for him.

MARVIN:
Hut!

(TRINA *hikes another ball.* MARVIN *drops it.*)

LADIES:
Pray for us all.

MARVIN:
Hut!

(TRINA *hikes another ball.* MARVIN *bobbles it but holds on.*)

LADIES:
But pray for the boy with the ball.

MARVIN:
There is something lacking in my play.
There are rules I must not be aware of.
If I touch her breast, would she applaud?
Would she protest? Appeal to God?
And weep?
If I touch her, would she let me fall asleep?

I touch her eyes, her lips are warm,
Her nose is much the same.
We're waiting for the whistle's sound.
She strokes my head and turns around.
I hear my name, then NAUSEA,
The game.

Love Me for What I Am

TRINA:
I met a man
In the can;
Wouldn't you know he was going my way?
We talked till four,
He talked more.
I was afraid I'd turn and say,

"Love me for what I am.
Not what I try to be

Love me for what I am, I am . . .
Someone imperfectly me."

The lights were low,
Don't you know, he gave a phony home address.
Then after weeks,
Guess who speaks:
"Darling," he says, and
I say, "Yes

"Love me for what I am.
Not what I try to be
Love me for what I am, I am . . ."
A person who likes to lie too much
I try too much
To impress other people.
Often my inferiors.

TRINA:
"Could you like a girl like
    that?
Could you like a girl like
    that?

Would you hold her in
    your arms?
Could you like a girl like
    that?"

MISS GOLDBERG:
Love, love
Love, love
SWEETHEART:
A person who likes to lie
    too much
I try too much to impress
    other people.
Often my inferiors.

ALL:
"Could you like a girl like that?
Could you like a girl like that?
Could you like a girl like that?"

TRINA:
We lay in bed
He plays dead. I play a recent 45.

He turns it low, talks so slow.
"Darling," he says. "We might survive.
Just love me for what I am.
Not what I try to be
Love me for what I am, I am
Someone imperfectly me."
    (A person who likes to lie too much.
    I try too much . . .
    Love, love, love, love.)
"Someone imperfectly me."

How America Got Its Name*

(MARVIN *is dressed as Columbus.*)

MARVIN (*speaking*):
Columbus didn't use to be a sailor. He was first and
foremost Director of Medicine at a prestigious institute
for doctors in Eldoro. That's the truth. But nobody
ever talks about his medical career anymore. 'Cause he
was embarrassed out of his job. Harassed. Made to be
the butt of jokes at medical conventions. This is what
happened. One day—this is the truth—one day outside
Poma del Fuego, he picked up a social disease from a
young man with red hair and broad shoulders like his
mother. By the time Columbus got to the Verona
Baths, no one could fail to notice an incredible diminu-
tion of intelligence on Columbus's part. He was half
insane by the time they strapped him to a ship, and
pushed him out to sea.

---

*"How America Got Its Name" was written in 1978, at least two
years before anyone had heard of a gay plague. What I was thinking of
when I wrote it, I have no idea. —William Finn

MARVIN AND LADIES:
Amer-ica.
God lives in America.

MARVIN (*speaking*):
With him on that boat were other socially diseased persons. From the few clippings extant, it appears they had a ball for half the trip and screwed like bunnies, never worrying if finally they were going to contract the dread disease. Because they all had it, you see—so they debauched the whole night and woke refreshed. This went on for thirty-four days.

MARVIN AND THE LADIES:
America.
God lives in America.
Where the grass is growing.
Where the sun is shining.

MARVIN:
Over the rivers.
Over the mountains.
Over the valleys . . .

LADIES:
We were working along the shore.

MARVIN (*speaking*):
"I am going to discover Cincinnati!" Columbus cried.
"Why 'Cincinnati'?" they asked him.
"For my aunt Cynthia and uncle Nathan," he said,
"who died four years earlier in a plague which my Institute never quite found the cure for. This is what the Jews do," he added, "name countries for the dead."

LADIES:
Cincinnati. Cincinnati.
Who would want to live in Cincinnati?
Cincinnati. Cincinnati.
Who would want to live in sin?

MARVIN (*speaking*):
Halfway out to sea, or on the thirty-fifth day, Columbus began to feel better. He stopped moaning in the
middle of lovemaking and began to say: "Hey! How
about that, young man?" or sometimes, boasting, "Tell
me you didn't like that!" Well, everyone was glad to
see Columbus becoming his old self again, but everyone
was also saying what a prick Columbus was. In his
diary he wrote: "Whatever it is I discover, it better
not give me any lip."

ALL:
Do they let you sing in America?
Do they let you laugh in America?
Do they let you write in America?
Do they let you fight in America?
Love. Love. Love.

Do they let you sing in America?
Do they let you laugh in America?
Do they let you write in America?
Do they let you fight in America?
Love. Love. Love.

MARVIN (*speaking*):
Fifty miles off Martha's Vineyard, it became clear that
everyone was cured, their brains restored, bodies once
again sound; and everyone had a good laugh about it,
maybe whistled with relief, maybe gave a few pecks on
the cheek here and there. But there was no heavy pet-

ting, you can be sure of that. "Hey, keep your hands off me, fella"—you heard that pretty often on deck. And then, later, "I said keep your hands off me!" Well, Lord knows, they spent many lonely evenings, clippings extant say, because each man feared acquiring the dread disease which had brought him there in the first place. In his diary Columbus posed the question: "How many passionate persons can fit comfortably on the head of a pin?" He pondered the question; he sat with his chin resting neatly in the palm of his hand, and he replied. Question: How many passionate persons can fit comfortably on the head of a pin? Answer: Merely one. Or, I don't know. I don't know.

LADIES:
There is little in way of   love—
We sail
Who can guess what we're thinking of?
We sail across the sea   MARVIN:
To find another land.   We sail.

There is little in way of love—
We sail   We sail.
Who can guess what we're thinking of?

ALL:
We sail across the sea to find . . .

MARVIN (*speaking*):
So there they were on board, looking out to see this new land Columbus was going to discover. And soon the blue horizon disappeared, to be replaced by a magnificent array of greens. *Fir* green, *ever*green, *lime* green, *dark* green, *light* green. The entire palette of greens stood maybe only a day's float ahead of them.

No one moved. No one was allowed to move. When they were maybe fifty or seventy-five yards away, Columbus could not withstand his enthusiasm any longer. "My land is so beautiful!" Columbus cried. "So beautiful!" they agreed in unison, like a chorus, like a barbershop quartet multiplied by fifteen. "So very beautiful!" There were tears in Columbus's eyes. "Men"—he turned to them, he looked at everyone straight in the face, he was very moved by his discovery—"men, no longer do I call this land Cincinnati; rather, this fine, green, beautiful land which I discovered today, I name America! After Amerigo Vespucci. A young man I met in Poma del Fuego with red hair and broad shoulders like his mother.

MARVIN:
God bless America
God bless . . .

MISS GOLDBERG (*with* TRINA *and* SWEETHEART *as backup*):
Hey, I love you. Set those sails.
A good man never fails.
Hey, I love you. Set those sails.
A good man never fails.

MARVIN (*speaking*):
The thing about explorers is, they discover things that are already there. Columbus closed his diary and went ashore.

Been a Helluva Day (Reprise)

TRINA:
Been a helluva day
Full of many surprises.
It's taken all of my will
To still stand high.
Marvin wrote me goodbye.
Filled it with details.
Explicit things that I can't try.
Says a good man never fails.
But me—
I let the cards fall where they may.

Time to wake up.
Time to wake up, Marvin.

Time I woke up,
And faced the day. . . .

Marvin Takes a Victory Shower

(*The* LADIES *stand behind* MARVIN *on chairs, showering him with watering cans.*)

ALL:
Scrubby dubby dubby
Look at Marvin take a shower
Look at Marvin in the tubby
Scrubby dubby dubby.
He is soapy with the soap he uses.
Everyone can see that he's a wet
Marvin boy.

MARVIN: SWEETHEART (*scrubbing him*):
Eyes and nose   Scrubby dubby
Neck and chest   Scrubby dubby
Groin and knees   Scrubby dubby
All the rest.   Scrubby dubby dubby dubby

ALL:
Scrubby dubby dubby dubby
Scrubby dubby dubby for Marvin.

MARVIN:
On my fourteenth birthday
Nothing was ready,
Nothing on the table, so I
Showed some wit.

MARVIN: LADIES:
And whaddya know?

                           What?

Whaddya know?

                           What?

MARVIN:
Whaddya no-
-body listened to me.
So I threw a fit.
And what do I mean?
I got my breakfast
The likes of which you've never seen.

LADIES:
And then what?

MARVIN:
I blew out the candles in a single breath
Then I thought of love,

Then I thought of death.
Then I made a deal,
The contents of which I cannot reveal.

LADIES:
All the ladies set their sails
And no one's home for Marvin.
All the ladies set their sails
And no one's home for Marvin.

MISS GOLDBERG:
My body is not yours to hold.

LADIES:
Our bodies are not yours to hold.
All the ladies set their sails
And no one's home for Marvin.

LADIES (*singing this over and over*):	MARVIN (*speaking*):
All the ladies set their sails And no one's home for Marvin.	Of course this is what I've wanted the whole time. But somehow . . . somehow . . . Please stop saying that. Please stop saying that. Stop it. Stop it. Stop it!

(*Silence.*)

MARVIN:
One, two, three, four.

LADIES:
Scrubby dubby dubby
Look at Marvin take a shower
Look at Marvin in the tubby

Scrubby dubby dubby
He is soapy with the soap he uses
Everyone can see that he's a wet
Marvin boy.

MARVIN:	LADIES:
Groin and nose	Scrubby dubby
Groin and chest	Scrubby dubby
Groin and knees	Scrubby dubby
All the rest	Scrubby dubby dubby dubby

ALL:
Scrubby dubby dubby dubby
Scrubby dubby dubby for Marvin.

Scrubby dubby dubby
Look at Marvin take a shower
Look at Marvin in the tubby
Scrubby dubby dubby
He is soapy with the soap he uses
Everyone can see that he's a wet
Marvin boy.

Scrubby dubby dubby dubby
Scrubby dubby dubby for Marvin
    (for Marvin) for Marvin
    (for Marvin)
Scrub (I love being) Dubby oooh
    (I love being)
Scrub scrub (I love being)
Scrubby dubby dubby dubby (I love being)
Scrubby dubby dubby dubby dub
    (I love being)
MARVIN.

Another Sleepless Night (Reprise)

ALL:
Another sleepless night alone in bed.
Another silent dawn.
You try to think of things you might have said,
You try to carry on.

SWEETHEART:
I wash my face.
Then drink beer.
Then I weep.
Say a prayer and induce
Insincere self-abuse
Till I'm fast asleep.

MISS GOLDBERG:
I've done too much talking.
That way I don't listen.
That way I don't hear a word you say.
Look, world, what I've found:
My eyes are gray, and the world is round.

MARVIN:
I know this girl.
I call her a girl.
She is my wife.
She is my thorn in the bushes.
No happy endings and no fuss.
What a girl, what a saint, what a fool ain't is my wife.
So I sleep in a bed too big for one person.
I'm big for one person.
But this bed is bigger than both of us.

LADIES: MARVIN:
Bored. Bored. Bored.   I know this girl.
  Bored.   I call her a girl, etc.

ALL:
Another sleepless night alone in bed.
The sun will fly, and does.
Another book you thought was best unread
Has proved indeed it was.

SWEETHEART:
I break a cup.

MISS GOLDBERG:
Scan a poem.

TRINA:
Then I eat.

MARVIN:
Shower up.

MISS GOLDBERG:
Strike a pose.

MARVIN:
Count my feet.

TRINA:
Count my toes.

SWEETHEART:
Till I'm fast asleep. Asleep. Asleep.

TRINA:
No one here to kick in bed.
No one here to rest my head against.
I am so alone in the middle of the night.

ALL:
I am so alone in the middle of the night.
Night. Night. Night.

In Trousers

MARVIN:
Four young ladies sat around and said they'd never
lose their love.
And then they lost their love.
Five good men in trousers banged a table when they'd
found their voice.
It was a ladies' choice.
The women sat demure and whistled through their
teeth;
They gave directions underneath
On legs and knees, these
Four young ladies sat around
And said they'd never lose their love.
And then they lost their love.

Jessie wore a bonnet, May a sash without a dash of
charm.
And Sis read *Commonweal*.
Bette was nervous so she picked a scab from someone
else's arm.
Then Jesse blew her meal.
They had a laugh, these women laughed their very
best.
The men in trousers aren't impressed.
Or else they're lazy.
Four young ladies sat around and said they'd never
lose their love.

Four young ladies sat around and said they'd never
    lose their love.
Four young ladies sat around and said they'd never
    lose their love.
And then they lost their love.

LADIES:
Baba dup ba dup ba dup ba dup
Baba dup ba dup ba dup ba dup
Ba da da . . .
Baba dup ba dup ba dup ba dup
Baba dup ba dup ba dup ba dup
Ba da da . . .

MARVIN:
Women sit like angels, men like vultures, it's a trifle
    crude.
It tends to make one think.
Same folk acting like from different cultures as they
    chew their food,
Completely out of sync.
It's simply this: four women and five men won't meet.
They must, for love, remain discreet—
And who's to blame them?

GOLDBERG:	SWEETHEART:	TRINA:
Marvin's giddy seizures.		
Marvin needs love.		
He needs love.		
He needs love.		
He needs love.		
He needs love.		
Marvin's giddy seizures.	Mar-	
Marvin needs love.	vin's	

He needs love.
He needs love.
He needs love.
He needs love.
He needs love.
Marvin's giddy
    seizures.
Marvin needs love.
He needs love.
He needs love.
He needs love.
He needs love.
Ahh!

Giddy
Seizures . . .

Mar-

vin's
Giddy
Seizures . . .

Ahh!

Marvin
Needs love.
Love.
Love.

Marvin
Needs love.
Love.
Love!

MARVIN:
Jesse works the corner near the drugstore,
May's a souvenir left on the bathroom shelf.
Bette wears fragrances like Eau de Wanting More
While Sis drank beer, and went and killed herself.
I was a young man once, in trousers, one of five.
I write to keep the pain alive. But ask no questions.
Four young ladies sat around and said they'd never
    lose their love.
Four young ladies sat around and said they'd never
    lose their love.
Four young ladies sat around and said they'd never
    lose their love.
And then they lost their love.

LADIES:
Baba dup ba dup ba dup ba dup
Baba dup ba dup ba dup ba dup
Ba da da . . .

MARVIN:
And then they lost their love.

LADIES:
Baba dup ba dup ba dup ba dup
Baba dup ba dup ba dup ba dup
Ba da da . . .

MARVIN:
Because we're dreaming in trousers,
Laughing in trousers,
Playing in trousers,
Making music in trousers,
Making movies in trousers,
Fighting in trousers,
Singing and dancing and writing in trousers,
People waiting in trousers,
People crying in trousers,
People living in trousers,
People screwing in trousers,
In trousers, in trousers,
In trousers.
In trousers.

Because we're dreaming in trousers,
Laughing in trousers,
Playing in trousers,
Making music in trousers,
Making movies in trousers,
People fighting in trousers,
People singing and dancing and writing in trousers,
People waiting in trousers,
People crying in trousers,
People living in trousers,
People screwing in trousers,
In trousers, in trousers,
In trousers,
In trousers.

(The lights fade.)

AFTERWORD

Discovering Family Values at "Falsettos"
By Frank Rich

The week that Vice President Dan Quayle began lecturing the country about family values, I decided to take my children—Nat, twelve, and Simon, eight—to a family musical on Broadway. Our options included:

- "The Secret Garden," a show about an orphaned girl who is raised by her widowed uncle.
- "Les Misérables," in which another orphan, the illegitimate daughter of a prostitute, is adopted by a bachelor who is never home.
- "Guys and Dolls," the story of a compulsive gambler and a nightclub dancer who have had sex without benefit of marriage for more than a decade.
- "Cats," which tells of a feline prostitute's aspirations to ascend to heaven.

All things considered, I decided that the most wholesome choice would be "Falsettos," the William Finn musical in which the hero, Marvin, sings in his first number of his overwhelming desire to be part of "a tight-knit family . . . a group that harmonizes."

The vice president might not agree. Though "Falsettos" offers such traditional family tableaux as a Little League baseball game and a bar mitzvah, it is set in an America where, as one song has it, "the rules keep changing" and "families aren't what they were." Marvin has left his wife, Trina, and his twelve-year-old son, Jason, for a male lover, Whizzer. When Jason's bar mitzvah arrives at evening's end, it is held in a hospital room where Whizzer is dying of AIDS. Those in attendance include a lesbian caterer of "nouvelle bar mitzvah cuisine."

Before I got the tickets, I told my children about all of the above except the one concept certain to defy their understandings, nouvelle cuisine. Did they still want to see "Falsettos"? Yes, they said, though Simon added that AIDS made him "very sad because it is an awful disease." Not so sad, however, that he would forgo the show. The boys' curiosity was piqued not only by my sketchy description but also by their knowledge that a relative of ours, my cousin's son Isaac, was playing Jason in a Washington production of "Falsettoland," the second of the one-act musicals brought together in the Broadway "Falsettos." If you like "Falsettos" in New York, I told Nat and Simon, we'll check out Isaac's "Falsettoland" in Washington as well.

When we took our seats at the Golden Theater on a Friday night, the boys were amused to find that they were the subject of stares, given that they were the only children in the house. They weren't self-conscious, but I was. Waiting for the performance to start, I had second thoughts. Should I have taken the easy way out and joined most of the country's other families that weekend at *Lethal Weapon 3*?

Then again, I had chosen to take Nat and Simon to "Falsettos" in part as an antidote to the monolithic images of masculinity with which they are routinely assaulted by television and movies. I do not believe, as the vice president does, that role models in pop culture determine what kind of adults children will become; if that were the case, my entire generation would resemble Lucy and Ricky Ricardo. Yet I wanted to take my children to an entertainment, a musical no less, that reinforces the notion that there are many ways to be masculine, from selfish to generous, from brutal to brave, and that it is up to each boy to make a choice. In this sense, "Falsettos" has more to say about becoming a man than some contemporary bar mitzvahs do.

I was also grateful to take my children to a show that depicts homosexuals neither as abject victims of prejudice or disease nor as campy figures of fun but as sometimes likable, sometimes smarmy, sometimes witty, sometimes fallible, sometimes juvenile, sometimes noble people no more or less extraordinary than the rest of us. In other words, gay people are just part of the family in "Falsettos", and the values of Marvin's family are those of any other. Marvin and Whizzer and Trina and Jason fight and fight and fight—not for nothing is the first song titled "Four Jews in a Room Bitching"—only to unite when one of them is in desperate need.

Such domestic images of gay people, and of gay people lovingly connected to heterosexuals, almost never surface in Hollywood movies or on network television, or in rock or rap music—the common cultural currencies of my children's (and most Americans') lives. They do exist frequently in the theater, but rarely in a piece so accessible to the young as "Falsettos." As co-written by James Lapine, whose other credits include the book of "Into the Woods." "Falsettos" hooks the audience on its unorthodox story as deftly as that Stephen Sondheim musical lured children into its subversive retelling of Grimm fairy tales.

Nat and Simon were riveted from the start, laughing in some if not all of the places adults did and taking in stride the show's PG-13 depictions of romantic homosexual intimacy in and out of bed. In Act II, they grew somber along with the characters, a change in key announced by the doctor's prognostic song, "Something

Bad Is Happening." As kids tend to do, they bounced back from grief faster than the grown-ups around them, leaping to their feet at the curtain call.

What did my boys take away from "Falsettos"? They liked the acting, the story ("I could never make up a story like that," said Simon, a prolific tale spinner), the jokes and the music. But they also responded to the show's family values. "Marvin tried to be a good father, and I think he was the best father he could be," said Nat, who added that he liked watching father and son work out their "adjustment" to a sudden change that was "hard to deal with at first."

Simon, who described the show as "very emotional," felt sorry for the "bummed-out" Trina but thought that Marvin had to leave her because "if you're gay, you shouldn't be married." He liked the fact that Jason, who "thought it was kind of weird that his father was gay," ended up "liking his father better" at the final curtain. If Simon had been in Jason's place, would he have liked Marvin's gay lover? "If he was nice, like Whizzer." Was he surprised to discover that the gay characters in "Falsettos" were the same in most ways as heterosexuals? "They *are* the same, Dad."

Both Nat and Simon were disgruntled that "Falsettos" had lost the Tony Award for best musical to "Crazy for You," which they dismissed as "corny." " 'Falsettos' is really about something," said Nat.

A week later in Washington, we resumed our conversation about "Falsettos" with Isaac, who is thirteen. While "Falsettoland" is Isaac's first professional acting experience, rave reviews and several weeks of capacity audiences at the Studio Theater have given him the self-assurance of a hardened theatrical veteran. He particularly delights in telling the story of the night the house was bought out by a gay and lesbian square-dancing group, prompting the stage manager to warn the cast in advance to expect a more idiosyncratic audience response. "We told him we could relate to the gay and lesbian," said Isaac, "but not the square-dancing."

Inevitably, Isaac's eight-year-old sister, Lilly, had insisted on seeing the show her brother had been rehearsing night and day. Her mother found a way to explain the show's characters, once Lilly noticed the similarity between a word she had recently learned in the second grade, "homophone," and "homosexuals," which is the first word sung in "Falsettoland." But "less than half" of Isaac's classmates had come to see him play Jason, and those who did were sometimes puzzled. One friend—"not my friend anymore"—told Isaac the next day in school that he had heard in the theater lobby that he was "a fag." Isaac chastised his friend for his language, then defiantly added, "I'm not a homosexual, but I work with numerous homosexuals!"

Isaac's own transformation into a knowing proselytizer for gay rights has been a fast one. Before "Falsettoland," he had never met anyone who was openly homosexual. In this he is no different from my sons, who do not know who, if anyone, among their acquaintances is gay. And Nat and Simon are no different from their father at their age, who, in another era not as distant as it seems, did not meet anyone until college who identified himself as gay and did not have an honest conversation with an uncloseted gay man until a couple of years after that.

Will a show like "Falsettos," or a dozen like it, sow tolerance, especially at a time when an exclusionary definition of "family values" is being wielded like a club in a divisive political campaign? I have my doubts. My children do not. While Nat and Simon were not sure if their friends would enjoy "Falsettos"—"they're not into plays"—they were, to my amazement, utterly certain that every boy they knew would be accepting of homosexuals whether encountered in theater or in life. (They were less optimistic about Vice President Quayle. Simon, who rated "Falsettos" ten on a scale of ten, said he thought the vice president, in light of the "Murphy Brown" episode, would give it a two.)

Surely not everyone they knew was so tolerant and free of the old sexual stereotypes, I insisted, but my children would have none of my adult pessimism. "*Kids* are stereotyped," said Nat, with an exasperated adolescent roll of the eyes meant to terminate the conversation. Since I believe in preserving tight-knit families as strenuously as both Marvin and Dan Quayle do, I conceded to my son that he was right.

July 12, 1992